ZACK IN ACTION

ZACK IN ACTION

by Beth Cruise

Collier Books
Macmillan Publishing Company
New York
Maxwell Macmillan Canada
Toronto
Maxwell Macmillan International
New York   Oxford   Singapore   Sydney

Collier Books
Macmillan Publishing Company
866 Third Avenue
New York, NY 10022

Maxwell Macmillan Canada, Inc.
1200 Eglinton Avenue East
Suite 200
Don Mills, Ontario M3C 3N1

Macmillan Publishing Company is part of the Maxwell Communication
Group of Companies.
Collier Books
First edition 1994
Printed in the United States of America
10 9 8 7 6 5 4 3 2

Library of Congress Cataloging-in-Publication Data
Cruise, Beth.
Zack in action / by Beth Cruise. — 1st Collier Books ed.
p. cm.
Summary: The Bayside High gang continues to have romance
problems, and Zack falls for an exotic Zoldavian transfer student
who may be a spy.
ISBN 0-02-041977-5
[1. High schools—Fiction. 2. Schools—Fiction.] I. Title.
PZ7.C88827Zab 1994
[Fic]—dc20   94-16641

To
all the
"Saved by the Bell" fans
who have ever had
romance troubles

Chapter 1

▲ ▼ ▲ ▼ ▲

DIIINNNGGGG!

"Luuunnnnccchhh!" Butch Henderson sang out. The fullback of the Bayside High Tigers leaned his head back on his beefy neck and bellowed like a moose calling his sweetie from across the frozen tundra.

Mr. Sandusky looked over his glasses. "I think we all heard the bell, Mr. Henderson," he said mildly. "Class dismissed. You may now tie on your feed bags."

A. C. Slater sighed as he closed his math book. He trailed behind the rest of the students as they picked up knapsacks and books and hurried out of the classroom. Once upon a time, Slater would have been leading the pack.

Lunch used to be his favorite subject at Bayside

High. He lived for the chance to scarf down lasagna in the noisy cafeteria while he joked about the latest hot gossip with his pals. But when *you* were the latest hot gossip, lunch was no picnic!

Slater slowly headed for the cafeteria. He had known from the beginning that falling for Kelly Kapowski wasn't his most brilliant move. She was his best friend's ex-girlfriend, after all.

But Slater had underestimated how dating Kelly could change *all* of his friends. The gang had always been tight, but with Zack Morris angry with Slater, and Slater's ex-girlfriend, Jessie, angry with Kelly, and Zack mooning over Kelly, and Jessie sighing over Slater, things were one big mess!

Slater swung into the cafeteria and spotted the gang at their usual table. It was Monday, and he knew what the topic of conversation would be: the weekend. He knew what was going to happen. He and Kelly would squirm and stammer and try to change the subject. Because that weekend they'd had their most romantic date ever.

"Greetings, guys," Slater said, dropping his knapsack on an empty chair.

"Hi, Slater!" Samuel "Screech" Powers greeted him. His frizzy curls looked extra springy today next to his polka-dot T-shirt and striped suspenders. "The special today is your favorite—tortilla casserole."

"It looked great," Lisa Turtle said, a mournful expression in her dark brown eyes. "But I'm on a diet. The Fool Moon Madness Masquerade Ball at the country club is coming up, and I have to fit into a very tight costume. I'm going as Catwoman." She picked up her fork and gloomily stabbed a piece of lettuce.

"Hi, Slater," Kelly said. Her deep blue eyes sparkled as she shot Slater a special smile.

"Hi, Kelly," Slater said.

Zack Morris looked up. He wished his submarine sandwich came equipped with torpedoes. He wished his best friend didn't have an incredibly muscular body and dimples as deep as the Grand Canyon. He wished he'd never lost Kelly Kapowski, and he wished he'd ace a midterm, just once. But this was real life, so he just chomped down on his sandwich and pretended it was Slater's head.

Jessie Spano looked up from her book long enough to nod a hello at Slater. He caught only a glint of hazel as her eyelashes lowered and she bent back over her book.

Slater didn't push it. He knew that Jessie still wasn't over his dating Kelly. He hadn't been going out with Jessie when he'd asked Kelly out, but Jessie considered that fact irrelevant. They'd been dating on and off for so long that Jessie couldn't help thinking of him as hers.

Slater dropped into his seat with a crash. "I brought my lunch today," he said, unwrapping his tuna salad sandwich.

"Tuna salad?" Lisa asked, looking over. "Since when do you eat tuna, Slater? You're a meat-and-potatoes guy."

Slater shifted uncomfortably. Kelly had made him the sandwich that morning when he'd dropped by to pick her up for school. It was her favorite tuna salad recipe, and she had looked so cute in her gingham apron that he'd sworn tuna was his new favorite thing to eat for lunch.

"I'm trying to improve my eating habits," he said defensively, and took a big bite.

"Red peppers and capers," Lisa said, studying the sandwich. "That looks like your special recipe, Kelly!"

Lisa's words hung in the air. Jessie fiercely flipped over a page, almost ripping it in two. Zack took a savage bite out of his sandwich.

Lisa wished she could stick one of her pink cotton socks into her mouth. Even if she *had* just bought them on sale. She just wasn't used to tension between her friends. Except for Slater, they'd all been together since kindergarten. Before, if someone had had a fight with someone else, they'd usually made up the same day. This tension had been going on for weeks now.

"So, um, what was everyone up to this weekend?" Lisa asked in a too-bright voice. "I was at the mall. What did I miss?" Lisa considered shopping a competitive sport, and she rarely missed "training."

"I had a fantastic weekend," Screech said. "I wrote a new program for my computer."

"I had a term paper to do," Jessie said. "And I played pool with Melissa Alden and some of her friends. Jeremy and Greg were there. They were a riot." She shot a look at Slater, but he was concentrating on his sandwich. She'd hoped the mention of the two cute boys would make him the teeniest bit jealous. But it looked as though it just made him more hungry.

"How about you, Zack?" Screech asked.

Zack pretended he was still chewing. He hadn't done anything over the weekend. Without Kelly, there was nothing he wanted to do. He didn't even want to *date*. This situation was totally and completely un-cool.

He took a sip of soda. Then he waggled his eyebrows mysteriously and summoned up the naughty twinkle in his hazel eyes that was his trademark. "The usual," he said.

"Whoa," Lisa teased. "I know what that means."

Screech nodded sagely. "Rented some movies, huh?"

Zack crunched down on a potato chip. What was the matter with Screech? Sure, everyone was probably perfectly aware of the fact that he was sitting around pining away over Kelly. But did the curly headed dweeboid have to *remind* them all the time?

"So what did you do, Kelly?" Lisa asked.

"Well," Kelly said, "let's see. I helped my mom do some housework Saturday afternoon. Sunday, I went to church in the morning, and then we had waffles for brunch. Sunday afternoon, I had a shift at the Yogurt 4-U, and—"

"What about Saturday night?" Lisa asked, forking up a bite of salad. "That's the crucial night of the weekend. Did you guys see a good movie or anything?"

"No," Kelly said. "We just . . . uh, had dinner out."

"Cool," Lisa said. "Where?"

"Café Romantique," Kelly said in a small voice.

"Wow," Lisa breathed. "Did you get one of those tables in the corner, overlooking the ocean?"

Kelly nodded.

"Jeff took me there once," Lisa said dreamily. "It's the most romantic restaurant I've ever been in. The pink tablecloths and the candlelight and the moon rising over the ocean . . . did you walk barefoot on the beach afterward?"

Kelly nodded. Her cheeks were tinged with pink. "Um, yes."

"That is so roman—" Lisa suddenly stopped. Now she *knew* she should shove her sock into her mouth. Both of them. Jessie was staring down at her book, her face red. And Zack looked like he was chewing on nails, not a sandwich.

"It was kind of cold," Kelly said quickly.

"We had to build a fire," Slater said. Then he gulped. Maybe he shouldn't have added that detail. It only made the evening sound even more romantic. But it *had* been romantic. Kelly had looked so beautiful with the firelight dancing on her sleek dark hair and lighting up her deep blue eyes. Still, maybe they should have said that they had gone to the library and been home by nine o'clock.

Zack choked on his soda. Jessie pounded him on the back.

"Dessert?" he choked out.

"Love some," Jessie said grimly.

The two of them walked toward the cafeteria line. "Do you believe them?" Jessie snarled. "It's Romeo and Juliet all over again. Frankie and Johnny. Fred and Wilma. Barney and Betty. Mildred and Newton—"

"Who are Mildred and Newton?" Zack asked, picking up a pack of chocolate-chip cookies.

"My next-door neighbors," Jessie wailed. "They've been married for forty-three years!"

"Relax, Jessie," Zack said, handing her the cookies. "Have some dessert."

"I don't want any," Jessie sniffed. "How can I eat when my heart is breaking?"

"Just consider it your just desserts," Zack suggested as he grabbed a piece of chocolate cake.

"Very funny, Zack," Jessie said. "I'll let you know when I start laughing."

"I mean it, Jessie," Zack said as he paid for their food. "Let's face it. We got what we deserved. We took Slater and Kelly for granted. We plotted behind their backs. I even tried to date another girl."

"What did *I* do?" Jessie asked. "I was loyal and honest."

"Let's see," Zack said, stopping and tapping a finger on his cheek. "There was the time you drained all the oil from his car and burned out his engine. And the time you almost married that guy Ramon so he could get a green card. And the time you kept on trying to prove your mom's boyfriend was a crook even though Slater asked you not to—"

"Okay, okay!" Jessie cried. "So I made some mistakes. But I *love* Slater, Zack. Doesn't that count for anything?"

"And I love Kelly," Zack said. "I'm hoping it counts for a lot. I want to win them back!"

Jessie eyed Zack hopefully. "I see a gleam in those eyes, pal. Are you coming up with a famous Morris scam?"

"Not yet," Zack said. "But I will. Until then, we have to hang tough. But we'll get them back again somehow or my name isn't Melvin Nudrucker."

Jessie couldn't help giggling. "You sure know how to inspire confidence."

When they approached the table, Screech was leaning back in his chair, smiling happily at Slater and Kelly.

"Now that's the way to keep the romance in a relationship," he said. "In my experience with Nanny, I know that there's no better way to a girl's heart than with a candlelit dinner. Of course," he amended quickly, "it *does* help if you don't set the tablecloth on fire."

Lisa giggled. "Or have the fire department ruin your girlfriend's carpet."

Screech waved his hand. "Nanny understands. She's the perfect girlfriend. And that's why we're perfectly happy!"

"But, Screech, you didn't even see her this weekend," Kelly pointed out. "Didn't you say you worked on your computer?"

Screech nodded. "Yes, but Nanny understands."

"When *was* the last time you went out with Nanny, Screech?" Lisa asked curiously.

Screech frowned. "Well, let's see. Maybe it was last Wednesday. No, last Wednesday, she had a *Bayside Beacon* meeting. Last Sunday afternoon? No, she had to visit her grandmother. . . ." He shrugged. "It doesn't matter. We're both busy. But I'm telling you, Nanny understands."

"Here comes Nanny now," Kelly said. "She looks pretty happy."

Screech straightened his suspenders. "You see? The magic never ends. Nanny!" he said, standing up. "I'm so glad to see—"

"Hi, Screech," Nanny said briskly. She turned to

the girls. "Listen, I've had the most fabu idea, girls. I was talking to Phyllis Ptowski last night, and she was complaining about not having anyone new to date. So I said, why don't you go after Tony Berlando because he broke up with Melissa Alden a month ago. And she said, no way, she didn't even know Tony that well because he's in the band and she has a tin ear. So, anyway, I had this great idea." Nanny paused dramatically. "I'm going to throw a Bring-Your-Old-Boyfriend Barbecue!"

"What's that?" Kelly asked.

"I'm inviting all the girls I know," Nanny explained. "And I'm asking each of them to bring an old boyfriend as a date. Then, at the party, everyone can mix and match. Who knows? We could start some new romances."

"That sounds like a great idea," Lisa said enthusiastically. "But how will I be able to choose which boy to bring? I have so many old boyfriends."

"How about Cal Everhart?" Nanny suggested. "Didn't you date him a couple of months ago?"

"Perfect!" Lisa agreed.

"And, Kelly, you can bring Zack. Jessie, you can bring Slater."

"Who are you bringing, Nanny?" Kelly asked.

Nanny grinned. "Screech, of course! Screech, are you free Friday night?"

Screech gulped. "I— I—"

"Great!" Nanny said. "Now, I'd better run. I've

got a zillion girls to talk to!"

Nanny dashed off, and Screech stared after her, his mouth open. He was Nanny's *old* boyfriend? How was it possible?

"Gosh, Screech," Kelly said, breaking the silence. "I'm really sorry."

Screech nodded. He had a lump in his throat, and he couldn't talk. It looked like Nanny *hadn't* understood. She hadn't understood at all!

Chapter 2

▲ ▼ ▲ ▼ ▲

Jessie almost flew home from school. She would swear that her feet didn't touch the ground. Not once.

She had a date with Slater!

Sure, it was because he was her *ex*-boyfriend. But at least she'd have a chance to spend time alone with him. At least he'd be coming to her house to pick her up, just like he used to. At least they'd be walking into a party together, arm in arm. Well, maybe not arm in arm. But *together*. Like they used to be.

Who could say that he wouldn't feel like he used to, too?

At home, Jessie sang her way through her chores. She dumped a load of laundry into the washer and cut up vegetables for her mother's pasta primavera. Then she grabbed the watering can and ambled out back to water the herb garden. She hummed the tune of a new ballad on the radio, occasionally bursting into song.

Zack's voice came from behind the hedge. "Do you mind, Madonna? I'm trying to study."

Jessie walked to the hedge and peered over it. Zack was lying in a lawn chair, his face tilted toward the sun. A glass of iced tea sat on the lawn next to his closed chemistry book. A sports magazine was opened up on Zack's lap.

"Who are you kidding?" Jessie said, laughing. "That chemistry book practically has cobwebs on it."

Zack gave her a baleful look over his sunglasses. "What do *you* have to sing about? I thought your heart was breaking."

"You've been in the sun too long, Morris," Jessie said cheerfully. "Don't you remember what happened today? I got a date with Slater! And you got a date with Kelly. Just think, Zack. Nanny's party is the perfect opportunity for us to reignite a few sparks."

Slowly Zack stood up. He pushed his sunglasses on top of his head and walked over to Jessie. He gazed at her with steely eyes. "No, it's not," he said.

"It's not?" Jessie repeated.

Zack shook his head. "You may *think* I was just catching a few rays before. But I was actually coming up with a foolproof plan."

"Fantastic!" Jessie burbled. "I just knew you

would. What is it? I'll do anything you say."

"Okay. Now, hear this—on your date with Slater Friday night, you'll act completely cool and distant," Zack instructed.

"*What?* I won't do it!" Jessie said, stamping her foot. "Zack, this is my big chance to win him back!"

"Hello? Whatever happened to 'I'll do anything you say'?" Zack asked.

"Anything you say that I *agree* with," Jessie amended.

"Jessie, listen to me," Zack pleaded. "I've given this a lot of thought. And what I've decided is this: When it comes to affairs of the heart, the tried-and-true methods are best. Old-fashioned values, Jessie!"

"What are you talking about, Zack?" Jessie asked suspiciously.

"That green-eyed monster, my friend," Zack said. "Jealousy! You're going to make Slater grind his teeth and howl at the moon."

"This is sounding better," Jessie said encouragingly.

"You're going to fall for someone else."

"But who?" Jessie asked. "There's no one I'm interested in. I only want Slater." She sighed. "Nobody compares with him."

"How about me?" Zack asked.

Jessie burst out laughing. "Y-you?" she choked.

Zack drew himself up stiffly. "Yes. And as soon as you stop laughing, I will explain."

"I'm sorry, Zack," Jessie said, wiping a tear from her cheek. "It's just that we've been best friends for so long. Who would believe us if we started dating?"

"How about Kelly and Slater?" Zack countered. "They were 'just friends' for a long time, and *they* started dating. Everybody believes them."

"True," Jessie admitted reluctantly. "But that's because they really are dating."

"If we're convincing enough, everybody will believe us, too," Zack said. "Look. Friday night is the perfect time for us to kick off our plan. We'll go out with Slater and Kelly, but we *won't* try to win them back. We'll be cool. That alone should drive them slightly nuts. Then, when we see each other at the party, we'll flirt like crazy. They'll go absolutely bonkers!"

"I don't know, Zack," Jessie said reluctantly. "Slater and Kelly know us too well. They'll know it's a ploy."

"No way," Zack said confidently. "We'll say that we followed their example and realized that having a friendship first was the way to go. If we do it right, we'll convince them. Besides, Jess, who's better at romantic sparks than Zack Morris? I practically wrote the book. I guarantee we'll be hot, hot, hot!"

Jessie leaned over and tilted her watering can over Zack. A few drops of water sprinkled out. "Hey!" he said, flinching. "What was that for?"

Jessie giggled. "Just wanted to cool you down,"

she said. "I want to make Slater jealous, not crazy. Okay, Zack. It's a deal. I'll see you Friday night, and we'll start stoking that fire."

Zack wiped at his arm with his T-shirt. "Just leave your watering can at home," he grumbled.

▲   ▼   ▲

On Friday night, it was still light when Nanny's barbecue began, but she had lit little votive candles in blue glass holders on the tables set up around the pool. The light from the flames twinkled as the shadows deepened on the lawn. Soft music wafted from speakers set up on the patio. Nanny had gone all out to create a romantic mood, and she had succeeded magnificently.

If only Jeff were here, Lisa thought dreamily of her current boyfriend. Things were going so great between them. Jeff was in college, but he still came back to Palisades every weekend. And even though he was usually busy with his big family, he always made time for Lisa.

"Wow, the place looks great," Cal said beside her. "Nanny seems so straitlaced at school. But she can throw a great party."

"It looks really romantic," Lisa agreed. She looked over at Cal. His brown eyes were sparkling, and there was an expectant grin on his face.

Lisa had forgotten how much fun she'd had when she'd dated Cal. He had a terrific sense of humor and had always been up for anything. Lisa had a tendency to wear people out, but Cal had always been ready for one more dance or a quick swim before lunch or whatever she had wanted to do. Why had she ever broken up with him?

Just then, Lisa caught sight of Cissy Garlock across the patio. That had been why, she remembered. Cal and tomboy Cissy had been next-door neighbors and best pals. So Cissy had tagged along on dates with Cal and Lisa, driving Lisa nuts. Lisa had decided that what Cissy had needed was a guy of her own, so she'd given her a makeover and urged her to go after the guy she wanted. Lisa had been shocked when the guy had turned out to be Cal.

But her problem hadn't actually been Cissy, Lisa thought now. It had been her pride. As soon as she had realized that Cal had returned a little of Cissy's interest, she'd let him go. Cissy and Cal's relationship had only lasted a few weeks. But once Lisa was through with a guy, she never went back.

But now, looking at Cal's handsome face, Lisa had to ask herself why.

It doesn't matter, Lisa told herself, giving herself a little mental shake. Now she had Jeff Racine. "Want a soda?" Cal said. "Or would you like to dance? Let's kick off the party. What do you say?"

"Sure!" Lisa said. She'd forgotten that with Cal, she'd finally met a boy who liked to dance as much as she did.

Cal swung her into a slow dance and began

singing in her ear. He didn't know the words, though, so he made up his own. He crooned:

> "Lisa, lovely Lisa,
> Over broken glass I'd crawl
> to see her at the mall.
> She wraps me around her finger,
> And I want to linger.
> Now, I know I'm no singer,
> But, boy, the girl's a zinger. . . ."

Lisa couldn't help laughing. She leaned back into his arms. "I didn't realize you were so musical," she teased.

"Oh, yes. I studied at the Tin Ear Conservatory of Music," Cal said gravely, a twinkle in his eyes.

Lisa felt her shoulder being tapped. "Oh, Lisa?" Nanny Parker asked. "Could you give me a hand with something?"

"Uh, sure, Nanny," Lisa said. She wondered why Nanny had picked her. There were plenty of girls standing around doing nothing. But she excused herself from Cal and quickly followed Nanny to the other end of the patio.

"What is it, hon?" Lisa asked. "Do you want me to dish up some salsa or something?"

"I want you to stop dancing with Cal," Nanny blurted out. Her hands twisted in front of her.

"What?" Lisa asked.

"Oh, I didn't mean that the way it sounded," Nanny fretted. "What I mean is, the whole reason I threw this party is so I could get to know Cal. I'm just crazy about him," she said wistfully, her eyes fixed on Cal. "We worked together on this feature article for the *Beacon*, and I don't think I've slept a wink since. He is so fabulous! Don't you think so, Lisa?"

Lisa shrugged. "Fabulous. No question."

"So if you dance with him all night, I won't ever get to talk to him!" Nanny said. She peered at Lisa behind her wire-rim glasses. "Oh, dear. You don't want him back, do you? I don't want to poach on your territory. But I know you're dating Jeff Racine."

"No, I don't want Cal back," Lisa said. She gave herself another little mental shake. "Of course I don't," she said more firmly. "But what can I do for you?"

"Can you give me some pointers on the way to his heart?" Nanny begged. "I really need help, Lisa. He doesn't notice me at school at all."

"Of course I'll help you," Lisa said. "I'm on your side, Nanny." Nanny was a sweet girl, and Lisa really liked her. And it was cute to see her all nervous and excited over a guy. But why did Lisa feel the teeniest bit reluctant to help her win Cal?

Lisa headed off to get a soda. Maybe it was just because she found it hard to let go of her ex-boyfriends. She always felt a sense that she owned a tiny piece of their hearts. But she was bigger than petty jealousy. Of course she'd help Nanny. Nanny and Cal would be perfect together. Almost as perfect as she and Cal had been.

▲   ▼   ▲

Zack and Jessie met on the far side of the pool. "Look happy to see me," Zack said through his teeth as he gave Jessie a grin.

"Why should I, you toad?" Jessie asked through a sweet smile. "I followed all your instructions. I was cool and distant. I didn't even say hello when he came to the door. I nodded. I practically sat outside the car. I pretended he was my great-aunt Clarice and acted really formal. I even asked how *Kelly* was, and he didn't notice a thing!"

"I had the same problem with Kelly," Zack admitted. He reached over to take Jessie's silk wrap. He kept his hands on her shoulders and looked deep into her eyes. "It's time for phase two," he said.

"Great," Jessie grumbled as she kept her eyes fixed on Zack and tried to put a simpering expression on her face. "Let's hope it works better than phase one."

Zack sneaked a peek over Jessie's shoulder. He sighed and his hands dropped.

"We might as well wait for our moment," he said. "They aren't looking."

Jessie twisted around. Kelly's head was pillowed on Slater's broad shoulder as they slowly circled in time to the music.

"I'll say," Jessie said woefully. "Oh, Zack, this isn't

going to work at all. They only have eyes for each other. They'll *never* notice us."

"Trust me," Zack said. "They will. We just have to be strong. By next week, Slater and Kelly won't be able to stand it, they'll be so jealous. They'll be begging *us* to take them back," he vowed. "I guarantee it. But we must keep our pact, no matter what. Deal?"

Jessie winced as Kelly smiled up at Slater and he bent down to kiss the tip of her nose. "Deal," she said.

Chapter 3

▲ ▼ ▲ ▼ ▲

Screech had hoped that even if Nanny *did* consider him her ex-boyfriend, he might be able to switch his status to "current" at the barbecue. But when he'd confessed to Nanny that he had missed her, even though he *hadn't* because he hadn't known she was gone, Nanny had just smiled vacantly and looked over his shoulder. And when he'd summoned up his nerve and told her he was still crazy about her, she'd kissed him on the cheek and told him he was sweet.

Screech sighed. Even though he wasn't super experienced in the girl department, he knew a kiss-off from a kiss.

He sat dejectedly on the little stone wall that circled the patio. He didn't want to eat. He didn't want to dance. He didn't even want a soda. He stared hungrily at Nanny and waited for her to notice him.

But why would she? he thought, sighing. He wasn't a football star like Slater. He wasn't a charmer like Zack. He couldn't play the saxophone like Tony Berlando or sing like Greg Tolan or make everyone laugh like Cal Everhart. There wasn't one single thing about him that stood out, even if he *was* wearing purple overalls and a yellow T-shirt.

The screen door opened, and Mr. Parker stepped out onto the patio. As soon as Nanny saw him, she broke out into a grin and ran over. Screech knew that Nanny worshiped her father. Stephen Parker was the editor in chief of the Palisades *Gazette*, and he and Nanny were super close. Nanny's favorite thing to do was sit around and read the Sunday papers with him. In the good old days, Screech had been invited over to join them.

Screech watched as Mr. Parker bent over and said something to Nanny in a low voice. Nanny nodded her head enthusiastically. "Of course!" Screech heard her say. "I'll get her."

A moment later, Nanny led out a girl who had a slender build and short dark hair. Even though he was completely prejudiced and thought Nanny was the cutest girl at the party, Screech had to admit that this new girl was beautiful. She had huge dark eyes and fair skin. There was something sad about her face, which gave her a mysterious air. She sure didn't look like she was from southern California. Here, it was practically against the law to walk around without a tan.

Nanny reached over and turned down the CD player. "Attention, everyone," she called. "We can get back to dancing in a minute. But I wanted to introduce you to a friend of mine. She's transferring to Bayside High on Monday, so I wanted everyone to meet her tonight. This is Irina Pastovic."

The girl made a slight, shy bow, and several kids around her said friendly hellos.

"Irina is from Karkasha, the capital city of Zoldavia," Nanny said. "I'm sure you all know that the country is in the middle of a civil war. Irina's parents are journalists, and they sent her over here to live with us. They met my father a couple of years ago when he was working in Paris."

"They consider Stephen Parker one of their closest friends," Irina said softly. She had a husky voice and spoke in soft, accented English.

Nanny slipped an arm around her. "And you're like family, Irina."

Irina smiled, and she looked more beautiful than ever. All the guys at the party moved a few steps closer.

"What's the current status over there, Irina?" Alan Zobel asked. "Is Karkasha still being bombed?"

Irina shook her head. "The cease-fire was declared on Thursday, and so far it is holding. But there have been cease-fires before, and they have all been broken by the Zervis. It makes me ashamed to be even half Zervi," she said softly, ducking her head.

"I'm afraid that here in America we get confused about what's happening," Tony Berlando said. "There's so much to keep track of."

Irina nodded. "It is a very complicated history my country has. Our tribal problems go back many years. And, it is terrible to say, but some of us there were brought up on hate."

"I was in Karkasha only five years ago," Mr. Parker said. "It was one of the most beautiful cities I had ever seen."

Irina nodded sadly. "Now there is little beauty left, I'm afraid."

"My grandmother is Zoldavian," Cal Everhart spoke up.

"Really, Cal?" Nanny asked eagerly. "I didn't know that."

"No reason why you should, Nanny," Cal said easily. "She's lived in America most of her life. But she says that the village where she grew up was almost completely destroyed by shelling."

"I'm sorry to hear that," Irina said.

"I tried to follow the war pretty closely in the beginning," Cal said. "But I have to admit that even I couldn't keep up."

Screech didn't like the way Nanny was gazing at Cal. Her mouth was slightly open, her head was cocked, and her eyes were shining. Or was that candlelight reflecting off her glasses?

"It's really not that difficult," Screech said, standing up. "The conflict escalated into a war four years ago when the Zervis began to shell the capital city. Then the Karpathis struck back, and smaller towns began to be involved. The Zervis had the upper hand from the start because they controlled the most territory and had the most weapons. After the United Nations got involved, the Zervis agreed to a cease-fire two and a half years ago. But that collapsed on Christmas Day, and the Zervis surrounded Karkasha and began shelling it. The siege lasted for fourteen months—until another UN agreement was signed. But that collapsed as well when the Karpathis retaliated for what they termed a massacre in the small town of Bilno. After four months of talks, the Zervis have agreed to another cease-fire, and everyone is hoping that this one will lead to peace."

Screech took a deep breath. The words had just tumbled out of him. He blushed, realizing that he'd been the center of attention. He took a step backward.

"Screech, that was the best thumbnail sketch of the Zoldavian conflict I've ever heard," Nanny's father said. "I wish the journalists on my paper could be as brief and concise."

Screech looked over at Nanny to see if she'd heard the compliment, but Nanny was edging over to talk to Cal Everhart, who had gone up to Irina. A small crowd surrounded the girl now, and it was mostly male. Screech drifted back and stepped on Mr. Parker's foot.

"Oops," Screech said. "Sorry, Mr. Parker. I didn't mean to do that."

"That's okay," Mr. Parker said. "I have another one. So, Screech, how long have you been interested in politics?"

"I'm not, especially," Screech said. "I just like to keep up with current events."

"We could use more of that attitude at the paper," Mr. Parker said. "Everybody's got their own narrow field of interest."

Suddenly, Screech had a brilliant notion. He almost felt like Zack. What better way to impress a girl than to get in good with the father she adores?

"Say, Mr. Parker," he said. "Did you mean that? About wanting more guys like me at the *Gazette*, I mean?"

"Sure, Screech," Mr. Parker said. "I wouldn't have said it otherwise."

"Well, I'd love to work there," Screech blurted. "For free. Just for the experience. Is there any kind of job I could do?"

Mr. Parker's light brown eyes narrowed behind his horn-rims. "Hmmmm. That's not a bad idea. One of our copy boys quit last week. We could use someone with your smarts and energy. I've always been impressed with your inquiring mind." His eyes twinkled. "As well as your pyrotechnics."

Screech smiled uneasily. He guessed that Mr. Parker still hadn't forgotten that tablecloth. "That would be super, Mr. Parker," he said. "When can I start? Tonight?"

Mr. Parker grinned. "Monday will be fine. Come see me after school, and I'll set you up."

"Thanks, Mr. Parker," Screech said. "You won't regret this, I promise."

Mr. Parker laughed. "I sure hope not, Screech."

Screech hurried over to Nanny, who was pouring tortilla chips out of a bag into a basket.

"Nanny, guess what!" he said. "I was just talking to your father. He offered me a job on the *Gazette*. Starting Monday, I'll be a copy boy on a real city paper!"

"That's great, Screech," Nanny said. She poured chips onto the floor as her gaze fixed on an area beyond Screech's shoulder. He turned and saw Cal eating barbecued chicken with Lisa.

Screech took the bag from Nanny's hand and poured the chips into the basket. "I know I can't expect much, at first. I guess being a copy boy is pretty lowly."

"You need more guacamole?" Nanny asked distractedly. "It's on the picnic table. Help yourself." She patted Screech's arm.

"No, I said *'pretty lowly,'*" Screech repeated. But

Nanny was already moving off toward the pool.

He sighed. He couldn't blame Nanny. She couldn't help being a little distracted. This was her party, after all, and she took being a good hostess seriously. She probably noticed that Cal and Lisa needed more potato salad. He'd talk to her about his new job on Monday. He knew she'd be completely impressed.

▲ ▼ ▲

Kelly swung her feet in the water as she watched the boys at the party crowd around a flustered Irina. She was glad that they were showing the girl some good old American hospitality. But she found it pretty funny that all the attention Irina was getting was of the male variety. And as usual, Zack Morris was leading the pack.

It wasn't that she was jealous. Not a bit. She was just . . . amused. And relieved. Because once upon a time, when she and Zack had been dating, she would have been sitting here cooling her sizzling heels in the pool while he paid court to a pretty stranger. And afterward, he would have said, "Aw, come on, Kelly. She's new in town. The least I could do was welcome her. You know you're the only girl for me. . . ."

Sure, Kelly thought. As long as a gorgeous stranger didn't come along. Or a group of cute tourists from Colorado when they were in Santa Fe. Or a pretty, blond-haired chef on their class trip to New York . . .

She sighed. "You know, Slater," she said, "I was

just thinking. It's so great to be at a party and not have to worry about my boyfriend leaving me for a beautiful stranger. Zack was terminally flirtatious, that's for sure. But you're a real gentleman."

Kelly turned to Slater, smiling. But he'd disappeared. He'd been lounging by the pool's edge right next to her just a minute ago.

Kelly's silky hair flew as she surveyed the pool. Then she looked over at the patio. Slater had joined the crowd around Irina!

▲   ▼   ▲

Fuming, Jessie headed for the kitchen. So much for her pact with Zack to make Slater and Kelly jealous. He'd dropped her like a hot fajita for the gorgeous Irina Pastovic.

The screen door banged shut behind her. Jessie saw Kelly at the sink, washing dishes. Leave it to Kelly to attend to chores during a party. The girl was so good that it was sickening.

Jessie moved toward the bottles of soda set up on the kitchen table. It was kind of awkward, bumping into Kelly here. They had been able to avoid being alone together for weeks.

"Hi," Jessie said. "I just came in for a soda."

"I just thought I'd wash a few glasses," Kelly said, setting one on the dish rack.

"That's nice of you," Jessie said through gritted teeth. She poured herself a diet cola and plunked several ice cubes in the glass. "But you always do the right thing, don't you, Kelly?"

She meant her tone to come out light, but she saw Kelly's cheeks flush an angry red. Or maybe it was because of the hot water.

Kelly rinsed a glass and set it in the drainer. "I try to, Jessie," she said softly. "Is there something wrong with that?"

"No," Jessie said, shrugging. "I didn't mean anything."

"It's a great party, isn't it?" Kelly asked.

"I'm having a fabulous time," Jessie lied enthusiastically.

"You and Zack seem to be having fun," Kelly said. Maybe *too* much fun. She'd never seen Zack and Jessie dance every dance together, or feed each other bites of potato salad. She had a feeling something was fishy, and it wasn't just the anchovy dip. She was having a hard time believing that Jessie and Zack were really interested in each other. They'd been best friends for too long.

And what about you and Slater? she asked herself worriedly.

"Zack is wonderful," Jessie said, trailing her finger in the wet ring her glass made on the table. "I never dreamed that . . . well . . . let's just say we're very good friends." Jessie peeked at Kelly from behind her curls. Was it working? She couldn't tell.

Kelly put the last glass on the dish rack and turned around. "Nanny's friend Irina seems nice. I guess she's been through a lot."

Jessie nodded. "Slater seems to find her fascinating," she said.

Kelly bristled. "What's that supposed to mean?"

"Well, I saw him rush over there," Jessie said. "I hope you're not jealous."

"Of course not," Kelly said stiffly. "I have nothing to be jealous about."

"Well, you never know," Jessie said. "Some girls don't respect the fact that guys are involved. They just move in. You know what I mean?" She gave Kelly a meaningful glance.

Kelly gasped. "That's not very nice, Jessie. You weren't with Slater when I started dating him."

"So, we'd broken up for about five minutes," Jessie said. "You sure didn't waste any time."

"Oh, come on, Jessie," Kelly said. "I've apologized and apologized. This thing with Slater just happened. And you know that he didn't want to go back with you."

"Slater *always* says that," Jessie said hotly. "That doesn't mean he means it! You didn't even give him a chance to change his mind. You just moved in and stole him away!"

"Jessie, I didn't steal him!" Kelly said, upset. "Things just happen sometimes."

"I know exactly what you mean, Kelly," Jessie said. "Because things just *happened* with me and Zack, too. We followed your example. And do you know what? It's the best relationship I've ever had!"

"Oh, right," Kelly said. "I'm super happy for you, Jessie."

Jessie chewed on an ice cube in frustration. She wasn't getting to Kelly at all! "Maybe you'd better get back outside," Jessie said archly. "You don't want Slater chasing *another* airhead."

"Airhead!" Kelly gasped. "Did you just call me an *airhead*?"

"Oh, I'm sorry," Jessie said. "What I meant to say was *bimbo.*"

"B-bimbo?" Kelly sputtered. "You're calling me a bimbo?"

Jessie took a sip of soda. She shrugged. "If the pump fits."

Kelly threw the dish towel on the counter. "And what do you think you are?" she said, her hands on her hips. "Who do you think is falling for this Zack-and-Jessie act? That's got to be one of the most lame-brain schemes you and Zack have ever pulled! And let me tell you, that's saying a lot!"

"It's not a scheme!" Jessie said, tossing her curls. "It's love!"

"You wouldn't know love if it came up and bit you on the nose," Kelly said. "You keep mistaking jealousy and infatuation for love, just like Zack! Come to think of it, you two deserve each other. You might get *A*'s in school, Jessie, but when it comes to real life, you flunk!"

Jessie stood up. Tears stung her eyes, but she'd never let Kelly see them.

"Kelly Kapowski, you're full of it!" she snarled.

"You're full, too?" Lisa cried, stepping into the kitchen. "I'm completely stuffed. I think I had three helpings of pasta salad so far." Suddenly, Lisa stopped. She looked at the two girls nervously. "Hey, what's up, you guys? Clue me in."

"Sure, Lisa," Jessie snapped. She grabbed her soda. "Here's an update for you. Kelly and I are history." She stomped out of the kitchen and banged the screen door behind her.

"That's right, Lisa," Kelly said. "My friendship with Jessie is over. Kaput. I'll never speak to her again!" Bursting into tears, Kelly dashed toward the bathroom.

Lisa looked around the empty kitchen. "Gosh," she breathed. "Was it something I said?"

Chapter 4

▲　▼　▲　▼　▲

Screech hurried to the *Bayside Beacon* offices first thing on Monday morning. He knew Nanny would be there. Ever since she'd been promoted from gossip columnist to features editor, she spent every chance she could at the school paper.

He knocked softly and pushed open the door. He expected to see Nanny sitting at the computer, or proofing copy, or doing another of the many tasks she did so brilliantly. But she was just staring out the window with a glazed expression on her face. Perfect! She wouldn't be distracted here.

"Nanny? Can I talk to you a minute?" Screech asked.

She turned to him in slow motion, a dreamy smile on her face. Then she blinked. "Screech! It's you! I was . . . thinking about someone—something—else. What's up?"

"I wanted to tell you something," Screech said. "I told you at the party, but I don't think you really heard me."

"Oh. Sorry. I guess I was pretty distracted, huh," Nanny said. She pushed her wire-rims farther up her nose. It was a gesture Screech knew well. His heart ached. How could he have thrown this relationship away without even knowing it?

This wasn't tickets to the Lakers game for him and Zack, or the check his grandmother had sent him for Christmas. When he'd thrown an important thing away before, everything had always turned out okay. But this time, he couldn't go through the trash and find it, like he had with the tickets. And he couldn't write to his grandmother for another one, as he had with the check. But he couldn't lose Nanny, either!

Nanny impatiently tapped a finger on her notebook. "Screech? What do you want to tell me?"

Screech had rehearsed what he'd planned to tell her. He'd wanted to sound mature and convincing and to say that he had decided to really take charge of his life and do something meaningful. But, instead, he just blurted it out.

"I got a job."

"With my dad. I know," Nanny said. She flipped open the cover of her notebook. "I heard you at the party. I'm real happy for you, Screech."

But she didn't say it right, Screech thought

despairingly. She said she was happy for him the way she'd say she liked catsup on her burger.

"You are?"

"Sure. Working at a newspaper is fun and great experience. My dad's happy, too. He thinks you're really smart." Nanny looked up at him. "Have you seen . . . Cal Everhart this morning?"

"Who?"

"Cal," Nanny said, looking down. Her light brown hair swung against her rosy cheeks. "I, uh, have an advance copy of that feature we worked on. I thought he'd like to see it."

"I haven't seen him," Screech said. He frowned. This wasn't the first time he'd noticed Nanny's interest in Cal. He could be pretty thick, but he wasn't *that* thick. So that was who his rival was!

"Oh," Nanny said with a sigh. "Is there anything else, Screech?"

"No," Screech said. "Nothing." He walked out and closed the door behind him. Now he knew what he had to do. Just getting the job wasn't enough. He had to become a great journalist. He had to crack a big story and get a byline.

There was only one question: Could he do it in time to get a date with Nanny for the Fool Moon ball?

▲　▼　▲

Zack was starting down the hall toward his locker when he felt his collar pulled tight. He was yanked backward, choking.

"Gggrrrhhhhaaaaa!" he gasped.

He felt himself being pulled back around the corner into the empty hall. Then he was whipped around. Zack met the worried hazel eyes of his partner in crime.

"We have to talk," Jessie said.

"I'll try," Zack croaked as he pulled at his collar. "As soon as my larynx returns to its normal size."

"They're on to us, Zack!" Jessie wailed. "Kelly told me she knew our flirtation was all an act." Jessie nibbled nervously at a fingernail. "I'm just not a very good actress, I guess."

"This *is* a delicate situation," Zack mused. "I guess it calls for a pro."

Suddenly, Jessie poked him hard in the chest. "And *you* didn't help any at Nanny's party, buster! You were practically welded to that girl Irina!"

"I was just trying to make her feel welcome," Zack said huffily.

"Don't give me that," Jessie said, waving her hand. "It didn't work on Kelly, and it doesn't work on me. You left me stranded at the party! Now, do you want Kelly back or not?"

"I'm sorry, Jessie," Zack said. "You're right. We have to follow through on this."

"Well, okay," Jessie said in a mollified tone. "I just found out that Kelly and Slater are playing tennis at the city courts today at four o'clock. I think we should have a tennis date, too. And we should have much more fun than they do."

"I catch your drift," Zack said. "It's a good plan. We'll act real surprised to see them there."

Zack caught a flash of a red skirt swirling around a terrific pair of legs. He looked over Jessie's shoulder. It was Irina! She looked prettier than ever in a simple skirt and a white blouse. Silver earrings dangled from her perfect little ears.

"So meet me at the courts at four," Jessie said. "Or should we drive up together? I—"

"Sure, Jessie," Zack babbled. "I'll meet you there at four. It will be perfect. Now I have to get to class."

"Okay," Jessie said grudgingly. "I have to get to home ec. But don't forget, Zack!"

"Forget what? Oh," Zack said. "Tennis. Right. Bye, Jessie!"

He ran around the corner just in time to see Irina consult a piece of paper as she surveyed the lockers. Zack hurried forward.

"Can I be of assistance?" he asked. "I'm Zack Morris. We met at Nanny's party."

"Of course. I remember you, Zack." Irina's dark eyes sparkled. "You're the one who brought me seventeen sodas."

"You said you were thirsty," Zack said, flashing a grin. "And I didn't know which one you liked."

"Now I have to find my locker," Irina said, frowning as she examined the paper. "But there are so many! Just like American sodas. It's very confusing."

Zack leaned over and looked at the number. "Number five-six-six. You're right down here, probably." He led Irina to the last locker in the row.

"Thank you, Zack," she said, opening it. "Everything is so new to me. I feel like a little baby, crawling around." She leaned closer. "Nanny had to get to school early today, so I came alone. I took the wrong bus three times, but don't tell anyone."

"I won't," Zack promised. He felt as if Jessie was yanking on his collar again. He was kind of dizzy. Up close, Irina's dark eyes and fair skin seemed to glow. He hadn't felt this way about a girl since . . . since . . . well, Kelly.

"Irina, could I show you around Palisades?" Zack asked. "It's a real easy town to get around in, once you get to know it. I'll show you the main roads and the beaches."

Irina smiled. "That would be wonderful, Zack. I'd like to get oriented here. Could we do it this afternoon after school?" She leaned forward to place her books in her locker, and perfume wafted toward Zack. It smelled like spices and musk, like nothing he'd ever smelled before.

"This afternoon would be perfect," he said dazedly. "I'll meet you right here."

Irina smiled at him and walked off. She moved like a dancer, Zack thought, leaning against her locker. He ran his hand along the metal door she had slammed. *I'll spend the whole afternoon alone with her,* he thought. *The whole afternoon . . .*

Zack straightened with a jerk. Jessie! He'd promised to play tennis with her at four!

He'd just have to think of an excuse. He couldn't give up his date with Irina. But he couldn't tell Jessie the truth. Not after what had happened at Nanny's party.

Zack groaned. Life just wasn't fair. He felt like he was cheating on his girlfriend, and he didn't even have one!

▲   ▼   ▲

When Jessie walked into home ec, she saw that her usual seat next to Lisa and Kelly was empty. Kelly's blue eyes were frosty as she caught sight of Jessie. She quickly looked away, as if she didn't care where Jessie sat. Tossing her head, Jessie took a seat on the opposite side of the room.

She opened her notebook and pretended to look over her notes while the class waited for Mrs. Miniver to appear. The bell rang, and Mrs. Miniver didn't show up. The class began to murmur. Mrs. Miniver was a control freak. She was never late.

A few moments later, Mr. Belding hurried into the room. "Sorry, class," he said. "Mrs. Miniver will not be in today. Or tomorrow. As a matter of fact, she's taking a little time off."

"What happened, Mr. Belding?" Kelly asked, concerned.

"Well, this weekend she was testing recipes for

you guys to try. She made some sort of salmon mousse thing, and she got food poisoning. She had to be rushed to the emergency room on Saturday."

The class gasped, and Mr. Belding quickly held up a hand. "She's fine now. She's just a little upset. So she decided to take a leave of absence until she got her confidence back."

Daisy Tyler raised her hand. "But, Mr. Belding, who's going to teach the class?" Her baby blue eyes were worried. Daisy took home ec very seriously. She had bashfully told the class that she was in training to become the perfect wife.

Since mostly everyone in the class had taken home ec for an easy grade, at first they all had thought she was pretty lame. But Daisy took diligent notes in her perfect handwriting and willingly gave copies to whomever asked. She soon had become the most popular student in class.

"Is the class going to be canceled?" Butch Henderson asked hopefully. He was the number one example of a student who took home ec for his only A. But thanks to Mrs. Miniver, he was barely scraping by with a C.

Mr. Belding shook his head. "Sorry, Butch. I've already found a substitute. Ms. McCracken from the Art Department will be taking Mrs. Miniver's place until she recovers."

Everyone exchanged pleased glances. Maisie McCracken was young and totally hip.

Mr. Belding poked his head out the doorway into the hall. Then he came back in, smiling. "And heeeeerrre's Ms. McCracken!"

Ms. McCracken strolled in. Her orangy hair curled around her small face, and her green eyes snapped with energy. She was wearing wide black pants with platform boots and an orange sweater. Instead of a belt, a chiffon scarf was pulled through her belt loops and tied in a big bow.

"Hey, gang!" she said, waving. "Thank you, Mr. Belding. I'm sure we'll all get along fine."

"Okay," Mr. Belding said. But he lingered by the doorway. "Are you sure I can't do anything to help? I make a mean tuna casserole."

"We'll be fine," Ms. McCracken said firmly. "Thanks again!"

As soon as the door closed behind Mr. Belding, Ms. McCracken turned to the class. "Now that he's gone, I have a confession to make. I can't cook or sew to save my life!"

Everyone in the class laughed except for Daisy. Her lower lip stuck out and wobbled.

"But w-what will we do?" she asked. "Mrs. Miniver was going to move on to hors d'oeuvres this week."

Ms. McCracken grinned. "Yeah, I hear her salmon mousse is a killer. You should thank heaven for small favors."

Daisy frowned. "Mrs. Miniver is an excellent

domestic engineer," she said haughtily.

Ms. McCracken boosted herself up to sit on the counter. "I didn't mean any offense, Daisy. I know Mrs. Miniver is top-notch. I've tasted her brownies. And I'm sure she'll be coming back to teach you before the semester's over. But until then, we're going to have to make do. So I was thinking: There's more to running a smooth household than cooking and sewing and all that. There's *feelings*. There's *family*. There's a bunch of people under one roof who have to get along. And that's how I came up with the plan for the next couple of weeks. We're going to do some serious sharing and consciousness-raising."

Jessie nodded, pleased. Ms. McCracken was right on her wavelength.

Daisy raised her hand. "What's consciousness-raising?" she asked doubtfully. "Do you need yeast? We weren't supposed to do leavened breads until May."

Ms. McCracken let out a bark of a laugh. "No yeast, Daisy. Just honesty." She clasped her hands and leaned forward. "Here's what we're going to do. We're going to explore our womanhood. We're going to get in touch with our feminine side and test our female power."

"Hey, wait a second," Walt Petronius said. "I'm just here for an easy *A*. I think I'd definitely flunk a womanhood quiz."

"Me, too," Butch Henderson said. "I don't have

any female womanhood to get in touch with. Believe me."

"Sure you do, Butch," Ms. McCracken said.

"Hey!" Butch said. "If you were a guy, I'd—"

"You see?" Ms. McCracken said. "Here you are, totally dependent on your masculine side. What you boys can do is get in touch with the feminine in you. It will do you good, I promise."

"I don't know about this," Walt said.

"It sounds gross," Butch said.

"Who knows? It could be the easiest A you ever made," Ms. McCracken said.

"Count me in," Walt said. "It sure beats having to master chicken Kiev."

"I never got an A," Butch muttered. "But I'll tell you one thing. No way am I going to wear pink."

Ms. McCracken laughed. "I won't make you wear pink, Butch." Now that she had the boys on her side, Ms. McCracken turned to the girls. "Here's what I thought we'd do. First, the class will discuss female rituals. Maybe we can come up with some ideas for projects. And we'll split up into groups of twos so that you'll have some up close and personal interaction."

Ms. McCracken reached for the class list. "Let me assign the groups before we start our discussion. Butch and Walt, you two deserve each other. Daisy and Melissa. Nanny and Lisa. Kelly and Jessie—"

"What?" Jessie blurted.

Kelly raised her hand. "Ms. McCracken? Jessie

and I can't work together."

Ms. McCracken looked over her paper at Kelly, then at Jessie. "You can't? Why not? I thought you two were friends."

"We *were,*" Jessie said. "Past tense."

Kelly blushed. "We're not really speaking, Ms. McCracken."

"I see," Ms. McCracken said slowly. "Well, that's perfect. You two can work out your problems through a traditional female ritual. The project will be a bonding experience."

"But, Ms. McCracken, we can't!" Jessie said.

"We can't even say 'Pass the sugar' to each other!" Kelly said. "This morning at the Max, my cereal tasted like cardboard!"

"This class would be a perfect place for the two of you to iron out your differences," Ms. McCracken said calmly. "Ha! *Iron* out! Home ec! Get it?"

Jessie and Kelly didn't smile. They glared at each other. Why work out their problems when they enjoyed hating each other so much? But Ms. McCracken had been firm. Even though she was hip, she was still a teacher.

"Help me out, class," Ms. McCracken said. "Can anyone name a female ritual Kelly and Jessie can work on together?"

Lisa raised her hand. "Adornment?"

"Perfect!" Ms. McCracken said. "Very good, Lisa. Kelly, why don't you change seats with Nanny and go sit next to Jessie. The two of you can try to come up with a few ideas."

Stiffly, Kelly rose from her seat and crossed the room to sit next to Jessie. While Ms. McCracken assigned the rest of the topics, the two girls conferred.

"So what do you think we should do?" Jessie asked.

Kelly shrugged. "I don't know."

"I guess I'll have to come up with something for us," Jessie said. Her tone implied that Kelly was too brainless to do so.

"But the topic is femininity, Jessie," Kelly said pointedly. "Something you know very little about."

Jessie glared at Kelly. Kelly glared back.

"How are you doing, girls?" Ms. McCracken asked, coming over to them.

"Not very well, Ms. McCracken," Kelly said honestly.

"Well, let's see if I can help. Kelly, is there something special you've wanted to do with your appearance lately?" Ms. McCracken asked.

"Well, I have been thinking about doing something different with my hair," Kelly admitted.

"Super!" Ms. McCracken said. "Jessie can help you with a new hairstyle. Jessie, how about you?"

"Well," Jessie said grudgingly, "I do need a costume for the masquerade ball at the country club."

"That's perfect," Ms. McCracken enthused.

"Kelly can help you with that. Okay, girls? You can both help each other to find new looks. Sound doable?"

"I guess so," Kelly said.

"I suppose," Jessie said.

Ms. McCracken walked off to help Walt and Butch figure out what "nurturing" was. Jessie and Kelly looked at each other.

"Well, when should we start?" Kelly asked. "This afternoon?"

"I have a tennis date with Zack this afternoon," Jessie said. "I'm not going to cancel that."

"That's okay," Kelly said. "I have a date with Slater, too. How about tonight?"

Jessie nodded shortly. "Fine. But listen, just because we're working together, it doesn't mean we have to like it."

"Fine," Kelly said. "It doesn't mean we even have to *talk* to each other."

"Fine," Jessie said.

Kelly tossed her head. "Fine."

Ms. McCracken came back over and beamed. "You see? I knew you two girls could work things out!"

Chapter 5

▲ ▼ ▲ ▼ ▲

Screech ran the last of the pencils through the electric sharpener. Then he carefully set them in the pencil holder on the city editor's desk. He arranged them in a line, points up, so that the editor would see what a meticulous job he had done. Maybe he'd realize that Screech would be the perfect person to go cover a six-alarm fire or something.

It had only taken Screech about fifteen minutes to realize that becoming a great journalist might take a little longer than a week. Being a copy boy meant that he swept the floor, fetched coffee from the deli downstairs, and kept the desks stocked with supplies. The men and women who worked on the paper barely noticed him. They were too busy clicking on their computer keys and dashing out to their assignments.

How was he going to impress Nanny this way?

"Nanny, I mopped the floor so clean at the *Gazette* that when someone dropped their bagel, they went right ahead and ate it without dusting it off first!"

Some accomplishment. That should really get her back, Screech thought sourly as he stacked a fresh pile of message pads for the receptionist. He picked up a broom and began to sweep up.

A reporter came out of the elevator and stopped to pick up his messages. He leafed through the little pink sheets. "Thanks, Rosalie," he said to the receptionist. "But next time, could you tell people I quit my job and moved to Tahiti?"

The receptionist smiled. "Feeling a little over-worked, George?"

The reporter leaned over the desk. "He's killing me, Rosalie. He's assigned me three different stories plus a three-part feature for the Sunday edition on the loss of government jobs in Palisades because of the end of the cold war."

Screech's broom stopped moving. He inched closer to the desk.

Rosalie gave George a sympathetic look. "Tell me about it. Jake is on the warpath, I hear. Can't you give something to Mike or Fran?"

George groaned. "They're snowed under, too." He shook a pink slip at Rosalie. "See this? This guy Barney Brill is calling to set up an appointment to tour this government remote sensing plant. Like I have time for this? I don't even know what it means. But Jake wants me to tour the place for atmosphere."

"Then you've got to do it, pal," Rosalie said. "Jake's the boss."

"Don't remind me," George said. "Catch you later, Rosalie." He walked past Screech into the noisy city room. Screech followed him, trailing his broom. George got to his desk and slipped out of his jacket.

"Um, excuse me. Sir? Sir?" Screech squinted at George's nameplate. "Mr. Smedley?"

"Yeah? What is it, kid?" George Smedley looked up at him.

"I'm the new copy boy," Screech said. "Samuel Powers."

"Hi, how are you. Hey—you're the guy with the mop! Let me tell you, I've never seen the floor so clean. I dropped a bagel on it and ate it, anyway!"

"I'm glad to hear that, Mr. Smedley," Screech said. "I'd like to *really* help out, though."

"That would be nice, kid," George said. "'Cause I sure could use it, let me tell you. Are you going on a doughnut run?"

"Not exactly," Screech said. "Here's my idea. I could do some of your legwork for you. Like touring the government plant. You could just tell me what to ask, and I could type up my notes and give them to you."

George eyed him with sharp blue eyes.

"Hmmmm. Have any experience with reporting?"

Behind his back, Screech crossed his fingers. "Tons. I'm like a fixture at my school paper." He *had* been a fixture—waiting for Nanny.

George slowly nodded. "Maybe we could do it, at that. You're on, kid. Let me type up a few questions for you, and you can head over this afternoon."

"Great!" Screech crowed. He rushed away to get his very own pad and pencil from the supply room. He was a real reporter! He just hoped no one would miss him in the city room. He didn't want to lose his job.

As he passed the city editor's desk, Jake Fallon let out a yell.

"Yeeeooooow!" he cried. "What lunkhead put my pencils with their points *up*? I could have stabbed myself to death!"

And on the other hand, Screech thought uneasily as he scurried past, *maybe it's a good idea to disappear for a little while.*

▲   ▼   ▲

Lisa had always liked Mrs. Miniver. When it came time for the sewing portion of home ec, Mrs. Miniver had proved that she took fashion seriously, even if her taste did run to horrible, shapeless frocks she called housedresses.

But Maisie McCracken was something else. Finally, Lisa saw completely eye to eye with a teacher. For Lisa's project, she got to go to the mall!

Ms. McCracken had assigned the topic of "courtship" to Lisa and Nanny. Nanny had been thrilled to have such an experienced dater as Lisa giving her courting tips. Lisa had decided that the very first thing they needed to do, even before researching some boring cultural rituals at the library, was shop.

Nanny needed an outfit for the masquerade ball. She had to completely knock Cal's eyes out and make him see her in a way he never had before.

Lisa strolled into the mall and took a sniff of her favorite scent: fashion products. Clothes. Makeup. Perfume. Accessories. Somehow, she caught a whiff of it all.

She saw Nanny waiting for her in front of the big clock in the center of the mall, and Lisa hurried toward her.

"We'd better get started," Lisa said as she came up. "We only have a couple of hours before dinner."

Nanny nodded. "Where should we start?"

"Well," Lisa said, "first of all, who are you think-ing of going as? The theme this year is television characters."

"And I've come up with a fabulous idea," Nanny said. She took a deep breath. "Lois Lane."

Lisa let out a shrill scream. "Are you delirious, girlfriend?"

"She's really smart and she's a reporter. She's always investigating an exciting story," Nanny protested. "And besides, Cal would be perfect as Clark Kent."

"But he doesn't want to date someone in a three-piece suit," Lisa said. "Let me think a minute." She gazed at Nanny while she puzzled over the problem. Nanny looked back hopefully. She was kind of cute, Lisa thought, in a mousy way. That was the problem. Her hair was light-brown and her eyes were brown and her features were regular. For a first impression, she was sweet, but maybe a tad on the boring side. She needed a little sizzle to get Cal to sit up and take notice.

Lisa snapped her fingers. "I've got it. Ginger from *Gilligan's Island.*"

"Ginger?" Nanny asked doubtfully. "You mean the redhead with that breathy voice?"

"Nanny, don't take the whole thing so seriously," Lisa advised. "The object is to attract Cal. Do you want to look interesting, or do you want to look sexy? If you go as Ginger, you can wear a red wig and lipstick and a tight sequined dress. If you go as Lois Lane, you can wear your glasses and sensible shoes." Lisa put her hands on her hips. "Which one do you want to be?"

"Ginger," Nanny said. "I guess."

"Then let's go." Lisa tugged on Nanny's arm and dragged her to her favorite store for evening clothes.

She flipped through the racks expertly while Nanny watched her in awe. In only minutes, Lisa chose a strapless gold-sequined dress with a sweet-heart neckline. "Try this," she said, directing her to the dressing room.

"Are you sure?" Nanny said, tripping after her. "It looks so . . . gaudy."

"Trust me," Lisa said. She pushed Nanny into the dressing room with the dress and shut the door.

In a minute, Lisa heard soft footsteps behind her. "Uh, Lisa? Are you sure about this?"

Lisa turned around and gasped. Nanny's shoulders looked creamy and the color of the dress picked up flecks of gold in her brown eyes. Not only that, Nanny had a *figure*. Cal was going to notice her—no question.

"Lisa?"

Suddenly, Lisa felt weird. She flung out a hand and grabbed onto a clothing rack. Nanny was smiling at her, but suddenly, it wasn't Nanny's face she saw. It was Cissy Garlock's.

It was déjà vu all over again! Here she was, fixing up another girl to win Cal's heart! *I must be out of my mind!* Lisa thought crazily.

Whoa, girlfriend, she told herself sternly. *Reality check.* What was wrong with fixing Nanny up with Cal? Lisa didn't want Cal. She had Jeff.

"Lisa? Do I really look that awful?" Nanny asked, dismayed.

"No, no," Lisa said quickly. "You look great, Nanny. You look absolutely gorgeous."

Nanny brightened and went over to look at herself in the mirror. Lisa tottered over to a chair and sat down. She didn't feel very well at all. But why should helping Nanny win Cal Everhart give her indigestion? That couldn't be what was making her so queasy. It was probably just the Chinese chicken salad she'd had for lunch.

▲ ▼ ▲

Irina leaned against the flagpole and looked out at the sparkling Pacific. "Thank you, Zack," she said. "I almost feel at home already."

"I had a great time," Zack said. It was true. He wouldn't have passed up this afternoon for anything. Thank goodness he'd thought of a good excuse to get out of playing tennis with Jessie. Everyone sympathized with a dentist appointment. He told Jessie that he'd forgotten all about it. She'd been disappointed, but she'd understood. Who didn't *want* to forget a dentist appointment?

"And it's not over yet," Zack said. "Why don't we go for a walk on the beach? We can walk to the pier and grab a snack."

A cloud passed over Irina's dark eyes, but she smiled at him. "I can't walk on sand very well. I still have some shrapnel in my hip. That's one reason my parents sent me here, to see doctors."

"Oh," Zack said. There weren't many times he was at a loss for words, but this was one of them. He really was a prize boob. He'd noticed Irina had a kind of spring in her step. He'd thought it was cute. And here he'd been walking her all over Palisades! "I'm so sorry," he babbled quickly. "You must be tired. We can sit down—"

"Zack! I'm fine," Irina said. Her dimples flashed at him. "I'm not a hospital patient. And a snack sounds great. Can we drive to the pier?"

"Absolutely!" Zack said, too cheerfully.

As they drove to the pier, Irina asked him about himself, and he found himself telling her about his father's new software company, about his mother's new painting classes, even about his breakup with Kelly. Irina was so easy to talk to.

They walked onto the pier, and Zack bought them each a hot dog and soda. Zack instructed Irina to put mustard, catsup, relish, and extra sauerkraut on hers.

"Trust me," he said, squirting more mustard on his. "You'll like it."

Zack laughed as Irina took the first bite and her eyes widened in pleasure.

"This is delicious," she said, as soon as she swallowed. She swirled a french fry in catsup and ate it. "It's so nice to eat in the open air," she said, looking out over the ocean. "Palisades is a wonderful place to live."

Zack looked at her as he took another bite. He realized that even as Irina enjoyed herself, there was still a hint of sadness to her. She was thinking of her country and the people she left behind. She couldn't completely enjoy food or warm weather or a beautiful day.

What must it be like, he wondered, to never be able to completely enjoy feeling happy? To always have to think of the people you love who are still living in danger? Zack knew that food and fuel were scarce in Karkasha, not to mention the ever present danger of being shot.

Irina only ate half her hot dog. She threw the rest in the trash can, saying she was full. But Zack knew she was thinking of her mother and father back in Karkasha.

"You must miss your parents very much," he said.

Irina nodded. "Yes," she said simply. "And I worry, of course. My father is a Zervi, you know. But he believes in peace. He's not popular with the Karpathis or the Zervis. I just hope the cease-fire lasts this time." She turned to Zack. "But let's not talk of it. What will you show me next?"

"There's a great park on the north side of town," Zack said. "There's a bandshell and swings and see-saws. There's fireworks there every Fourth of July, and concerts every Saturday night during the summer."

"Very American," Irina said. "I'd like to see it. Perhaps I'll be here this summer."

I hope so, Zack thought to himself as they strolled down the pier. He wondered if it would be okay to take Irina's hand. He knew they'd made a connection that day. But he wasn't sure if she liked him as much as he liked her. Maybe she only thought of him as a super-friendly tour guide.

He still wanted Kelly back. But if he *couldn't* have Kelly back, he'd like to get to know Irina better. He'd like to create one perfect moment for her without the tiniest hint of sadness. He'd like to hear her laugh without seeing that little bit of melancholy in her eyes.

Zack looked at his watch. "Hey, I have an idea. It's only four-thirty. After we see the park, let's drive by some of the old Victorian houses in that area. They're really neat."

Irina stopped and put a hand on his arm. "It is four-thirty?"

"Just barely," Zack said. "It's still early."

"I must go, Zack." Irina turned to him and flashed a quick, nervous smile. "Thank you again for this perfect afternoon. I must run."

"But I can drive you—"

"No."

"But where are you—"

"I must go. Good-bye, Zack."

It happened so fast he barely had time to react. But Irina was walking briskly down the pier, away from him. Puzzled, Zack turned to throw away his soda. And that's when he saw Jessie.

By the look in her blazing eyes, he knew she'd

seen him with Irina. So much for his dentist appointment. He waved at her halfheartedly, but she didn't wave back. She stalked toward him and put her hands on her hips.

Zack smiled at her nervously. "Would you believe it, Jessie," he said. "Irina's not just a transfer student. She's a dentist!"

Chapter 6

▲ ▼ ▲ ▼ ▲

Screech could tell that Barney Brill was surprised to see such a young reporter. But the guy was warm and friendly. He showed Screech all around the plant and constantly threw out statistics off the top of his head, which kept Screech scribbling furiously as he tried to keep up.

The tour ended in the last building, all the way at the end of the parking lot. Barney waved at the guard and led Screech past a sign that read CLASSIFIED: AUTHORIZED PERSONNEL ONLY.

Barney paused outside a door and punched a few numbers. The door buzzed, and he pushed it open. Screech saw a stairway leading upward.

"Sorry about this," Barney said. "The elevators in this building are being fixed."

"No problem," Screech said.

But the stairs turned out to be a slight problem for Barney. He puffed his way up them and had to pause on each landing to catch his breath.

"My wife keeps telling me to exercise," he told Screech with a smile. "But this elevator problem has finally convinced me."

He pushed open the door to the third floor.

"The end of the cold war hit us hard," he said. "It really cut into our productivity. But we still do satellite surveillance of trouble spots."

"Do you have good security here?" Screech asked.

Barney nodded. "Top-notch. You'll notice I keyed in my code on a pad downstairs. No one can get up here without his or her code."

Screech looked down at his pad. "Can you give me an idea of how accurate your equipment here is?" he asked.

Barney grinned. "Sure. A couple of years ago, we were mapping the Bering Sea by satellite when this submarine emerged from the water. We saw the captain come out on deck."

"Wow," Screech said. "You mean you can see *people* from way up in outer space?"

Barney snorted. "That's nothing. We saw that the guy was having something hot to drink, and we knew he was drinking *tea*. You know why? Because we saw that little paper square that's on the end of the string."

"Wow," Screech breathed. He really was impressed. He quickly scribbled down the story. It was just the kind of thing George would be looking for, he guessed. George had told him to be sure and get "the human element," even if the guy was a complete "techno-head."

Barney showed him around the third-floor offices, where much of the mapping, called remote sensing, was done. Then he puffed his way down the stairs again. He paused at the entrance to the building.

"You mind if I don't walk you out?" he said with a grin. "My office is on the first floor, and there's a jelly doughnut waiting for me in it. It's my reward for climbing those stairs."

"I don't mind at all," Screech said, reaching out to shake his hand. "Thank you for the tour, Barney. It was very interesting."

Screech pushed open the door and started down the stairs to the parking lot. He didn't think this story would set Palisades on fire, but George could probably make it interesting. At least Screech had done more today than sharpen pencils. And when the feature came out, he'd be able to tell Nanny that he'd done research for it. That would be better than nothing.

Screech paused at the entrance to the parking lot. Where had he left his car?

Just then, he saw a figure hurry through the

parking lot and into an alley that ran alongside the building. The petite woman walked quickly, almost furtively. Something about her looked familiar, too.

Screech inched around the corner. The woman was walking down the alley. She stopped and looked up, shading her eyes with her hand. Quickly, Screech ducked behind a palm tree.

The woman looked at her watch. Then she reached down and picked up a handful of dirt. She tossed it at one of the windows on the third floor.

Screech watched as the window opened. He couldn't see who was there. All he saw was a forearm. The arm waved at the woman, and then dropped a manila envelope down into her waiting hands. It was just like in the movies!

The woman waved up at the window and turned around. At last, Screech got a good look at her face. Now he knew why she'd seemed familiar. The woman wasn't a woman—she was a girl. She was Irina Pastovic!

▲   ▼   ▲

That night, Kelly heard her phone ring after dinner. She knew it was Slater, and ran to answer it. He usually called her every night now, even if they'd seen each other in the afternoon. It was really sweet of him to give her so much attention. But tonight, she wished he hadn't called at all. They'd played tennis this afternoon and had said good-bye only a few hours ago.

It wasn't that Kelly didn't want to talk to him. It was just that . . . well, she'd like a night off. When had Jessie had a chance to do anything if she was on the phone with Slater all the time? she wondered.

"Hey, momma," Slater said when he heard her voice. "What's new?"

"Not much," Kelly said brightly. "Just some macaroni-and-cheese casserole. I just had dinner."

"Yum," Slater said. "We had chicken and rice. Now I've got to hit the books. I just wanted to check in."

There was a pause. Kelly knew what was coming next. Slater was going to bring up tomorrow night. They'd talked about seeing a movie. But Kelly had changed her mind. Things were so weird at school with Jessie angry at her. Everything felt all mixed up. It wasn't that she didn't want to see Slater. She just didn't want to see him so much.

"About tomorrow night," Slater said. "I was thinking. My schoolwork has been taking a nosedive. Would it be okay if we took a rain check?"

"No problem," Kelly said quickly.

"So I'll see you tomorrow, okay?" Slater said. "I have wrestling practice early, so I can't drive you to school."

"That's fine," Kelly said. "I can get a ride from my brother. Or take the bus. I'll see you there."

Kelly heard the doorbell ring downstairs. She knew it was Jessie. She was coming over to "adorn"

Kelly by giving her a new look. They'd already decided to shampoo red highlights into her hair.

She heard the sound of the front door opening
and her mother greeting Jessie. "Go on up, sweetie,"
her mother said.

"Slater, I have to run," Kelly said. "I, uh, have to
do my homework."

"Duty calls," Slater said. "Have a good one, Kelly.
I'll see you tomorrow."

Kelly hung up. That was all she needed, to have
Jessie walk into her room and hear her talking to
Slater!

Jessie walked into the room carrying a small
shopping bag. "Hi," she said offhandedly.

"Hi," Kelly said. Her voice came out a little too
bright and squeaky. It was just too weird to be doing
this with Jessie when they were scarcely talking to
each other.

"I talked to Lisa," Jessie said. "She gave me this
recipe from this new book she got called *Secrets of
Mother Nature*. It has all these shampoos and creams
you can make yourself from natural ingredients. Lisa
gave me one for this rinse called burnished brunette.
It will give you these great red highlights. I already
mixed up a batch." Jessie reached into the bag and
took out a jar with green glop in it.

Kelly eyed it nervously. "Are you sure it won't be
too intense?"

"No way," Jessie assured her. "Lisa said that the

look will be totally subtle. And if you don't like it, it will shampoo out in about six shampoos."

"Okay," Kelly said. "Let's give it a try."

"Let's do it over the sink in the bathroom," Jessie suggested. "Your hair needs to be wet."

In the bathroom, Kelly leaned over and rinsed her hair in the sink. Jessie put on plastic gloves and started scooping the mixture into Kelly's hair. "If you do want the color to be a little more intense, you can wrap your hair in a warm, moist towel," Jessie advised. "It takes about twenty minutes."

Jessie worked the glop into Kelly's hair. Then she dunked a towel into warm water and squeezed out the excess. Kelly wrapped her wet hair in it.

"Now we have to wait," Jessie said.

"Well, let's go back to my room," Kelly suggested.

In her bedroom, Kelly sat on the bed. Jessie took the hard desk chair. Jessie examined her nails. Kelly cleared her throat.

"Do you want to watch TV while we wait?" she asked Jessie.

Jessie looked relieved. "Sure."

Kelly clicked on the television. She was afraid that Jessie might argue with her about what show to watch, but their favorite nighttime soap was on. It was so engrossing that they forgot when twenty minutes were up.

Kelly sprang to her feet. "It's been forty minutes!" she said. "I'd better rinse this out and dry my hair."

"I'll tell you what happens," Jessie said, her eyes glued to the TV screen.

Kelly ran off into the bathroom. Jessie turned up the volume. Would Brad find out that Monique was cheating on him *and* stealing his company?

"What a sleaze," Jessie said to the TV. Then she heard a high-pitched scream.

Jessie turned down the volume. Funny. That sound hadn't come from the TV.

She heard the scream again. It was coming from the bathroom! Jessie sprang up and ran down the hall to the bathroom. She rattled the knob.

"Kelly? Are you okay?"

Slowly, the door opened. Kelly stood there, the towel still in her hand. Her mouth was open. Her blue eyes were wide. And her hair was bright green!

Chapter 7

▲ ▼ ▲ ▼ ▲

Kelly pointed a shaking finger at Jessie. "Y-you!"

"Me?" Jessie squeaked.

"You!" Kelly yelled.

Jessie had never seen Kelly so angry. Her face was bright red. Next to her green hair, she looked almost . . . Christmassy. Jessie stifled a laugh. She was sure Kelly wouldn't appreciate the observation.

"You're *happy* it came out like this!" Kelly accused her. "I saw that smirk, Jessie Spano. You did this to me deliberately!"

"No, Kelly!" Jessie protested. "I wasn't smirking. I swear. I don't know how this could have happened. I followed Lisa's directions exactly."

Kelly looked in the mirror and let out a fresh wail. "I don't believe you!" she said. "You're too meticulous and Lisa's too careful for this to happen. You *wanted* me to look like this! You're so green with envy about Slater, you can't stand it!"

"Gee, Kelly," Jessie said. "If you ask me, *I'm* not the one who's green."

Kelly's mouth opened. No sound came out. She pointed to the door. "Out," she croaked.

"Kelly, I—"

"Out!" Kelly screamed. "And never darken my door again! I hate you, Jessie Spano!"

▲ ▼ ▲

The next morning, Zack was making toast and pouring himself a glass of juice when he heard a knock at the kitchen door. Screech stood outside, his nose pressed to the screen. At least he thought it was Screech. He was wearing a trench coat, sunglasses, and a hat.

Zack looked down and saw a pair of zebra-patterned basketball sneakers. "Hi, Screech."

"Shhhh," Screech said.

"Come on in," Zack whispered.

Screech opened the screen door a few inches and slipped inside.

"Want some breakfast?"

"No, thanks. Zack, I've come on a mission."

Zack spread some peanut butter on his toast. "No kidding. Juice?"

"No, thanks. Not while I'm on duty," Screech said. "Zack, I have to talk to you."

Zack crunched into the toast. "I'm all ears, Screech."

Screech sat down at the table. "We've been friends a long time."

"Yeah," Zack agreed. He eyed Screech's getup. "Sometimes I think too long."

"Thanks, Zack. I feel the same way. That's why I thought I could come to you," Screech said. "I know it's not fair to ask you to do something like this on the basis of our friendship. But that's why I'm here."

"Do what, Screech?" Zack asked.

"And I wouldn't ask if I didn't know where else to turn," Screech said.

"It's okay, Screech," Zack said. "Just ask."

"It could be dangerous—"

"*Ask!*"

"And the future of our country could be at stake."

"Screech," Zack said calmly, "if you don't ask whatever it is you want to ask me, I'm going to dip you in peanut butter and roll you all the way to Bayside High."

Screech took a deep breath. "I want you to date Irina Pastovic."

"You want me to *what*?" Zack asked.

"I know, I know," Screech said fervently. "I know you're trying to get Kelly back. But, Zack, there's a good reason. And it's spelled the good ol' US of A."

"What are you talking about?" Zack asked impatiently. "What does the future of our country have to do with Irina?"

Quickly, Screech outlined what he'd seen. "I'm positive it was her," he finished. "She signaled some-body, and they threw down a top secret document."

"How do you know it was top secret?" Zack asked skeptically.

"Because it came from the classified section of the plant," Screech answered. "And why else would they be acting so weird? They were acting like *spies*, Zack."

Zack crunched down thoughtfully on his toast. It all sounded far-fetched to him. Screech had probably gotten something wrong, as usual.

"So will you do it?" Screech asked solemnly. "I know it's a lot to ask."

Date Irina? Date that gorgeous, charming, mys-terious, sexy exchange student? The very thought made his heart sing. It made him weak in the knees. It made him want to shout out loud.

Zack sighed. "All right, Screech. I'll do it."

Screech sighed. "What a guy. Your country will appreciate the sacrifice, Zack."

"It's the least I can do," Zack said.

▲　▼　▲

Kelly had washed her hair three times after Jessie had left and three times that morning. The green hadn't faded one bit. Every time she looked in the mirror, she reminded herself of the creature in *Alien Planet*.

"Look at it this way," her older brother Kerry said. "At least you're going to a *masquerade* ball on Saturday. You can go as mold."

Leave it to an older brother to make you feel worse, Kelly thought despairingly as she headed down the hallway at school. Lisa had loaned her a bunch of adorable hats, but she was still miserable.

Kelly swung into home ec a few minutes before the bell. She hoped that Ms. McCracken would turn up early. There was absolutely no way she'd continue working with Jessie on the project. She'd even show Ms. McCracken her hair if she had to.

Luckily, Ms. McCracken breezed in before the bell. Kelly hurried up to her.

"Hey, Kelly," Ms. McCracken said. "Cute hat."

Kelly touched the brim of the black straw hat she was wearing. "Thanks, Ms. McCracken. There's a reason I'm wearing it."

Ms. McCracken nodded sympathetically. "Bad hair day?"

"Worse than that," Kelly said in a low tone. "Jessie turned my hair green, Ms. McCracken! She was supposed to give me auburn highlights for our project. And she turned it green!"

"Oh, dear," Ms. McCracken said.

"She did it deliberately, Ms. McCracken," Kelly said. "I can't work with her anymore. You have to split us up."

"I *didn't* do it deliberately," Jessie said defiantly,

coming up from behind Kelly. She stood with her feet planted slightly apart and crossed her arms. "And *I* won't work with someone who calls me a liar!"

Ms. McCracken looked from one to the other. "I can see we have a problem," she said. "Kelly, why don't you believe that Jessie didn't do it on purpose? It's unlike you not to give someone the benefit of the doubt."

"You didn't see the triumphant smile on her face when she saw me," Kelly said.

"It wasn't triumphant," Jessie said. "It wasn't even a smile, hardly. It's just that you looked . . . well, funny."

"You two girls have been friends a long time," Ms. McCracken said. "It would be a shame to break up your friendship over something like this. Kelly, I think you owe Jessie another chance. And, Jessie, I think you owe Kelly an acknowledgment of her feelings. She has a right to be upset. And both of you can explore these issues in the next part of your project. What are you doing for Jessie, Kelly?"

"I'm making her costume for the masquerade ball this weekend," Kelly muttered.

"I'm going as Jeannie from an old TV show, *I Dream of Jeannie*," Jessie said enthusiastically. "It's this really old show, Ms. McCracken. Practically ancient history."

"I remember it well," Ms. McCracken said dryly.

"Oh," Jessie said in a small voice.

"Good move, Jessie," Kelly said in an undertone. "Get her on our side."

"I'm looking forward to your project," Ms. McCracken said to them. "And I don't want to hear any more nonsense about not working together. You two are going to find a way to work together—or flunk!"

Kelly glared at Jessie as she stalked back to her seat. She'd make Jessie's costume. She'd do a good job, just to show that she was a superior person. But she'd never forgive Jessie for what she'd done. Never.

▲ ▼ ▲

Slater saw Jessie in the hallway heading to the cafeteria. He hurried to catch up to her.

"Great move, Spano," he said. "Just because you're green with envy, did you have to turn Kelly's hair that color?"

"I didn't," Jessie said, turning to him. "And leave it to Kelly to go crying to you about it! That wimp!"

"She didn't," Slater countered. "I accidentally knocked her hat off. Luckily, there was no one else around. She told me what had happened after I stopped screaming. How could you do that, Jessie?"

"I didn't do it on purpose," Jessie said evenly. "And I'm tired of being accused of it. Why don't you go find Kelly so you can hold her hand?" She quickened her pace.

"When are you going to grow up?" Slater asked her, hurrying beside her. "When are you going to be honest and talk about your feelings instead of just getting mad all the time? That's what broke us up."

Jessie stopped in her tracks. "Oh," she said. "Silly me. I thought *Kelly* broke us up."

"You see! That's just the problem," Slater exclaimed. "You can never admit that something might be wrong with *you.*"

"That's not true, Slater," Jessie said quietly. "You know I came to you and apologized about not being straight with you. And that I admitted that I could be too competitive with you. But I swore to you that I'd change. You never gave me a chance."

"Oh, I gave you a chance," Slater said. "And then we went to Santa Fe and you blew it. You spent all your time on a wild-goose chase instead of repairing our relationship. *That* was the last straw, Jessie."

"I know," she said, tossing her ponytail over her shoulder. "And what happens with me and Kelly is none of your business. So what are you doing here right now? Why don't you just leave me alone?"

Slater bit his lip. He *didn't* know why he couldn't leave her alone. He didn't know why he still thought about her. He didn't know why he couldn't just be happy with sweet, wonderful Kelly. Maybe he just liked torturing himself. He was a football player, wasn't he? He was used to getting slammed around until his head swam. Dealing with Kelly and Jessie didn't feel much different.

"You're right, Jess," he said in a level voice. "I'll leave you alone."

Slater walked away. As soon as he turned the corner, Jessie burst into tears.

Screech came down the stairs. "Don't worry, Jessie," he said, coming up to her. "I know you didn't dye Kelly's hair green deliberately."

"Thank you, Screech," Jessie sobbed.

Screech tugged at his curls. "But do you think you could do it again? I need a new look, too. Something that will really stand out. I think Kelly's hair looks great. It's the same color as my iguana!"

Chapter 8

▲　▼　▲　▼　▲

On Wednesday evening, the blaze of the setting sun turned the Pacific into molten turquoise. The sand changed from honey yellow to dark gold as the sun slipped into the sea. In-line skaters on the concrete walkway cast long shadows.

Zack eased out of his backpack as he sat on a bench and stretched out his legs. "This is my favorite time of day," he said.

Irina faced into the sun. The orange light licked at the ends of her dark, feathery hair. "I can see why," she said. "It's so warm and quiet. Serene in the middle of all this violent color."

"Exactly," Zack said. Somehow, Irina captured his feelings in words and images that he never would have thought of.

Irina laughed as she stretched out a leg and

regarded her skates. "I know just what Nanny would say if she'd seen me this afternoon. That I stunk on wheels." She pronounced the American slang in an awkward way that Zack found charming.

"I thought you were very graceful as you were falling," he told her with mock earnestness. "Your hip's okay, isn't it?"

Irina threw back her head and laughed. "You are much too charming, Zack Morris," she said in her husky voice. She sighed. "Yes, my hip is fine, but I am way too tired and thirsty to skate anymore."

"I'll get us some water," Zack said. He skated over to the concession stand and bought two bottles of spring water. By the time he got back, Irina had taken off her skates and slipped into her loafers.

He gave her a bottle and tapped his against hers. "What shall we drink to?" he asked jokingly.

Irina looked out over the water. "Peace," she said simply. She tapped her bottle against his and drank.

How can this girl be a spy? Zack thought. *Screech must have seen someone who looked like Irina.*

Irina stared moodily out to sea. "That's all I wish for, Zack," she said. "Peace. I remember when I would wish for a new blouse, or a book, or for my parents to let me go on vacation with my best friend, Naida. Everything I wished for was personal, something for me. Maybe peace is, too."

"Where is Naida?" Zack asked. "Is she still in Karkasha?"

"Naida is dead," Irina said. "She was killed by a sniper."

Zack gasped. "I'm so sorry, Irina. That's terrible."

"Yes," she said. "It is."

She turned to him. "I had a wonderful afternoon, Zack. Thank you."

"But you're not leaving?" Zack said. "I thought we'd have dinner. Something real American, like pizza."

Irina smiled. "Some other time, okay? I have to go."

"I'll take you—"

But it was the same as last time. "No," Irina said, shaking her head and standing up. "I'll see you at school tomorrow."

And a moment later she was gone, running lightly down the walk toward the parking lot. This time, Zack was determined to follow her. He got up quickly to run to his car, but he forgot he was wearing his skates. His feet went out from underneath him, and Zack crashed to the concrete.

"Way to go, dude," a blonde teased as she skated by.

Zack crawled to his feet. Grabbing his backpack and the skates he'd borrowed for Irina, he skated toward the parking lot. He zoomed across the asphalt and practically rammed into his Mustang. Then he hurriedly unsnapped the skates and jumped into the driver's seat. Screech would kill him if he found out he'd blown this opportunity. And he'd kick himself if he lost the chance to prove Irina was innocent.

Zack started the car and cruised out of the parking lot. He drove carefully, keeping an eye on the street. He didn't want Irina to see the car, but he didn't want to miss her.

Then he saw her up ahead at the bus stop. A bus was just pulling in, and Irina hopped aboard. She looked distracted and in a hurry.

Zack let a car go in front of him. Then he followed the bus. It was a local bus that stopped every few blocks, and it was hard to keep behind it and not hold up traffic.

The bus traveled from the west side of Palisades through downtown, and then headed south. They passed a few factories and small businesses. Zack started to get nervous. He had a feeling he knew where Irina was headed. Could it be that Screech was right? Had he really seen Irina at the plant?

Irina got off the bus at the last stop and hurried inside the gates to the government plant. Zack parked the car a little way down the street and followed. It was quitting time, making it easy to keep Irina in sight without her seeing him.

Irina hurried past the first building to the one at the end of the parking lot. She stayed in the shadows as she ignored the entrance and kept walking toward the side. Zack waited until she'd passed underneath the trees and turned the corner. Then he hurried after her.

Irina was looking up at the building. Then she glanced at her watch. She reached into her purse and took out a small penlight. She flashed it up at the windows.

A moment later, a light flashed three times. Zack counted the windows from the front. The signal had come from the fourth window on the third floor. He watched as the window slowly rose. Then a man's hand came out. The man made a thumbs-up sign, but Irina was too far away for Zack to see her expression. The man dropped an envelope down, and Irina caught it.

She turned toward Zack, and he melted back into the trees. His heart was pounding, and his brain buzzed in disbelief. If he hadn't seen it with his very own eyes, he never would have believed it.

Screech was right. Something fishy was going on. But could gentle Irina Pastovic really be a spy?

▲　▼　▲

When the phone rang after dinner, Kelly ran to answer it. She hadn't spoken to Slater practically all day.

"Hi, Kelly," he said. He sounded a little subdued. "How's it going?"

"Fine," Kelly said. "Are you okay? You sound different."

"Just beat," Slater said. "Wrestling practice." He

paused. "I didn't tell you. I talked to Jessie."

Kelly twisted the phone cord around her finger. "You did?"

"I told her what a lousy thing she did, dying your hair green," he said. "Of course she denied it. It was kind of nasty."

"Oh," Kelly said. "I'm sorry, Slater. Maybe you should just stay out of this feud."

"That's what I decided," Slater said with a sigh. "So, do you want to get together Friday night? I've got tons of homework, but—"

"I have tons of homework, too," Kelly said.

"Maybe we should talk later about going out, then," Slater said. "We might want to skip it. We're going out Saturday, anyway."

"Right," Kelly said. "That's a good idea. We'll talk later."

"Okay," Slater said. "I'll catch you at school tomorrow, momma. I can't wait to see your next hat."

Kelly laughed. "Thanks. I'll see you tomorrow."

She hung up the phone thoughtfully. There had been a weird difference in Slater's voice tonight, and she wasn't sure what it was. Probably the talk with Jessie had bothered him more than he let on.

Kelly went to her mother's sewing room. The green gauzy material for Jessie's costume was already cut out and waiting to be sewn. Nanny had designed the pattern. It would only take her a few hours to put it together.

Kelly sat down at the sewing machine and pulled the material toward her. Things were so mixed up, she thought with a sigh. Half the time she didn't know what she thought or felt—about Jessie, about Slater, about Zack. She knew that her feelings were intense. If only she could figure out *what* they were!

Was she jealous of Jessie and Zack? And if she was, did that mean she still loved Zack? And if she did, did that mean she should be with him?

Kelly bit her lip as she basted a hem. She had to admit it. She was totally wigged out at the thought of Jessie and Zack together. But she still wasn't sure if they really were together. It would be just like Zack to try to make her jealous. How could she find out the truth? She needed a plan.

Kelly stopped sewing. The answer was so simple that she'd laugh out loud if she wasn't so miserable.

She'd just ask him!

She knew Zack so well. She knew when he was lying to her. And even if he didn't tell her the truth, she'd know what the truth really was.

▲   ▼   ▲

Zack called Screech that night and told him what he'd seen. He said he'd keep sticking close to Irina. But Screech knew that he had to look at the problem from another angle. He had to get back inside the building.

Screech called Barney Brill at his office and

caught him just as he was leaving.

"Samuel Powers from the *Gazette*," he said crisply. "I have a few more questions for the article, Mr. Brill. I'd like to come down and take another look around."

"Sure, no problem," Barney Brill said.

"Is four o'clock tomorrow okay?" Screech asked.

"Four o'clock, ten o'clock, three o'clock, it's all the same to me," Barney said. "Just don't come on my lunch hour."

▲   ▼   ▲

The next day, Screech met Barney at the front desk promptly at four. "So, what do you need to know?" Barney asked amiably as he signed Screech in.

"Well, nothing specific," Screech improvised. "You gave me all the numbers the other day. This is a think piece. I'd just like to soak up the atmosphere. Especially on the third floor, where the remote sensing is done," Screech said. "I'd like to get the feel of all that knowledge. That was really fascinating."

"Sure," Barney said. But his face fell.

"You don't have to come up with me," Screech said quickly. "I know it's quite a climb."

Barney broke out into a smile. "Great. I'll just buzz you in, then." He led Screech back to the last building, past the security guard, and punched out the numbers on the keypad. When he stepped back, Screech was so close he bumped into him. "You must be eager to get started. Go right on up. You can come by my office afterward if you have any more questions."

"Thanks, Barney," Screech said gratefully. He pushed open the door and dashed up the stairs to the third floor. Zack had said that the signal had come from the fourth window from the front. Orienting himself, Screech hurried down the hallway.

All the office doors were closed. Screech stopped in front of the fourth office. Then he paused. What if each office had two windows? Or one had three or the other had two, or one? Screech scratched his head in puzzlement. What would Zack do? *Zack* was cut out to be an investigative reporter, not Screech!

Screech squared his shoulders. No more negative thinking, he told himself. That wouldn't get anything accomplished. Nanny wanted a hero, not a sniveling coward who gave up.

He walked back to the first office, knocked, and then stuck his head in. Three men were bent over a computer screen. One of them looked up.

"Oops," Screech said. "Sorry."

Two windows. Screech went to the second office. He knocked and popped his head in. A woman in glasses was clicking computer keys. One window.

"Sorry," he said. "Guess I want next door."

She nodded without even looking up.

Screech's hand trembled a little as he knocked on the third office. Unless it didn't have any window at all, this was the office. This was where the spy was.

"Come on in!"

Screech opened the door. A young man dressed in a sweatshirt and baggy corduroy pants was standing in the middle of the room. He held a nerf basketball in his hands. He tossed it over Screech's head. "Two points!" he chortled.

Screech looked above the door. The basketball hung gently in the hoop.

"Congratulations," Screech said. "Did you win the game?"

"It's only halftime," the guy said, grinning. He stuck out his hand. "Mark Quigley."

"Samuel Powers," Screech said. "I'm doing a feature article for the *Gazette.*"

"On this place?" Mark asked in disbelief. "It's pretty dead. We've had so many layoffs in the past two years."

"That's the slant of the article," Screech said.

"I guess that's good," Mark said, doubt creeping into his voice. "But it won't help the unemployed folks much. Their skills are too high-tech for most of the jobs around here. Most of them have moved north to Silicon Valley."

Screech wondered if Mark was trying to throw him off the scent. But he seemed so open and friendly! Screech couldn't figure it out.

He thought he should ask a reporter-type question. "Are you afraid of being laid off?"

Mark shrugged. "Who isn't? But despite that basketball hoop, they do keep me busy. Remote sensing
is still an important field, no matter if there's a cold
war or not. It's still an unpredictable world." Mark
leaped up and grabbed the basketball. "And I have
family in Palisades. I don't want to have to leave."

"Do you work a full day?" Screech asked. "I
mean, what are your hours, if you don't mind my asking?"

"Technically nine to five," Mark said. "But I'm
usually here until seven."

So he was probably still around when Irina came
by. Once it was at five. The second time had been at
six-thirty.

"What's your specific area of expertise?" Screech
asked.

Mark shrugged. "It varies." He grinned at
Screech. "Besides, I'm not allowed to tell you."

Screech looked down at his notebook, but no
brilliant questions occurred to him. Mark sure
didn't seem like a dastardly spy. Screech didn't
know what he had been expecting. A confession? A
codebook to fall out of his pocket? A beautiful
blonde in the closet?

"Well," Screech said, "I'd better let you get back
to work."

"Good luck with the article!" Mark called. His
next ball swished into the hoop.

Screech closed the door with a sigh. Was Mark

the one who'd dropped the envelope to Irina? Or had someone else used his office? But how could Screech possibly find out who? He was at a dead end.

Chapter 9

▲　▼　▲　▼　▲

Zack had an early-morning track practice on Friday. If there was one thing he hated, it was getting up even earlier than usual and running around a track before he was awake. But for some reason, Coach Sonski thought it built character. The coach was also a morning person.

"Lift up those feet, Morris!" he bellowed. "You're not skating, you're running track! At least, that's the rumor!"

Even if Zack was awake enough to think of a cute rejoinder, he was too out of breath to say it. So he waited until Coach Sonski had headed back into the locker room for more juice. Then Zack jogged over to the bleachers to collapse.

He bent over and tried to get his breath back. *Why* had he ever signed up for track? It was probably to impress some girl back when he was a fresh-man. Now he couldn't remember who. Meanwhile, he'd been running in circles for four years.

"Zack? Can we talk a minute?"

Zack looked up. Kelly stood there in front of him, morning-fresh and glowing. She bit her lower lip, a sure sign that she was nervous.

"Okay," he panted. "At least, *you* can talk. I'll lis-ten. Give me a chance to catch my breath."

"Sorry to interrupt practice," Kelly said, sitting down next to him.

"I'm not," Zack said. "What's up?"

Kelly twisted the hem of her skirt. "Well. I know what I'm going to ask is really none of my business. It's taken me a whole day to work up the nerve to talk to you."

Uh-oh, Zack thought. Conversations that started this way always seemed to end up with him in the doghouse.

"And you don't have to answer," Kelly said.

"What is it, Kelly?" Zack asked cautiously.

"But we were really close once," Kelly said, her blue eyes pleading, "and I guess I'm counting on that so you'll give me an honest answer."

"Kelly, you're worse than Screech," Zack said. "Just ask me."

"Are you and Jessie really seeing each other?" Kelly blurted. "Or are you just pretending to make Slater and me jealous?"

Zack felt a thrill of triumph. It had worked! Kelly was jealous!

But then he hesitated. He hadn't expected his plan to boomerang back in his face like this. He hadn't expected Kelly to take the honest approach and *ask* him about it. She was supposed to steam silently and then fall into his arms.

He hated when people took the honest approach.

Because then he felt as though he should be honest back.

And hadn't he and Kelly broken up because he hadn't always been honest with her? Hadn't he promised to never, ever lie to her again?

But he and Jessie had sworn a blood pact. Neither one of them would admit the truth. If he admitted the truth to Kelly, Slater would find out, and Jessie would be furious. Did he owe more to Jessie or Kelly?

It was an impossible question. But Jessie had a meaner right hook.

Zack looked into Kelly's eyes. He knew that he had to make this the most convincing lie he'd ever told. If he lied now, Kelly could never, ever find out that he and Jessie hadn't had a brief romance. If she did, she'd never trust him again.

"It's true, Kelly," he said in a quiet voice. "Jessie and I are involved. We started out to console each other. But then . . . things changed."

"Oh," Kelly said in a small voice. "I can understand that."

"We didn't mean for it to happen," Zack said. "But then we saw you and Slater. We saw that it could work. And you know what? It *does*. You can be best friends and date, too. Everything is so easy and natural."

Kelly gulped. Zack was saying all the things she had said to him—about Slater! She didn't realize how those words could hurt.

"It could become pretty serious," Zack finished. "I think I owe it to you to tell you that."

"Are you really, truly sure, Zack?" Kelly asked. "Is Jessie the one for you?"

Zack nodded. "We're not dating anyone else. We're seeing where this takes us."

He peeked at Kelly. She was gazing over the track field. There was a glaze in her eyes. Was it tears? Zack didn't want to hurt her. But maybe this would make her see that she still loved him. If that happened, the end would justify the means. They would all be happy again. These past few weeks had been murder for everyone.

"Gosh, Zack," Kelly said woefully. "I'm really happy for you."

She didn't look very happy. She looked like she'd been run over by a truck. "Thanks, Kelly," Zack said. "I know you mean that."

"I do," Kelly said. "I'm just a little surprised, that's all. But I know you'd never lie to me. I know that you—" Kelly stopped abruptly. She shaded her eyes with her hand and looked up.

Irina had come up without Zack seeing her. She stood, smiling down at him.

"Good morning," she said. "Sorry to interrupt."

"No problem," Kelly said amiably. She was glad for the diversion, actually. "How's it going, Irina?"

"Fine. I just came by, Zack, to tell you I might be a few minutes late for our date tonight," Irina said. "I have to help Nanny with her costume."

"That's okay, Irina," Zack said, stealing a glance at Kelly. "Really. Don't worry about it."

"Okay," Irina said. "I'll call you and let you know what time."

"Fine," Zack said nervously.

Kelly watched Irina walk off. Then she stood up. "I have to go now," she said tightly.

"Kelly, let me explain." Zack said. "Irina and I aren't dating behind Jessie's back. I mean, we *are* going out, and Jessie doesn't know about it. But it's not what you think."

"Stop right there, Zack. I've already seen this movie," Kelly stormed. "And you have nothing to explain to me. For the first time, I feel sorry for Jessie." She turned around and stomped off.

Zack was up to his old two-timing tricks, all right, Kelly thought furiously. All that talk about dating Jessie—and he was seeing Irina at the same time! Now she remembered why she'd fallen out of love with him in the first place. Jessie was welcome to him!

Kelly banged open the door to school. She must have been crazy to think . . . to think . . . *whatever* she'd been thinking!

▲ ▼ ▲

Nanny looked all over school for Lisa. She really wanted to talk to her before classes began. She checked the locker room, the gym, the outside stairs, and the cafeteria before she realized where Lisa must be.

She burst into the girls' room on the first floor. Lisa was leaning forward toward the mirror, holding up two tubes of lipstick toward the light.

"What do you think, Nanny?" she asked. "Tremulous rose or Scallop-shell pink?"

"Pink," Nanny said. She leaned against the sink next to Lisa. "Can you talk and primp at the same time?"

"Don't insult me, girlfriend," Lisa said. She waved her lipstick airily. "I'm a pro. What's on your mind? If it's private, you'd better check the stalls."

Nanny leaned over. "All clear." She popped up again. "It's about Cal."

Lisa's hand jerked, and the pink lipstick streaked across her cheek. "Guess I'm not the expert I thought," she muttered. She dampened a tissue and scrubbed at her face.

"Lisa, this courtship ritual is going nowhere," Nanny complained. "I gave Cal a soulful look yesterday, just like we practiced, and he asked if I was feeling sick. I complimented him on his cool sneakers, and he looked at me like I was crazy. Then I realized he was wearing boots. I guess I should have checked first."

"That's key," Lisa agreed.

"It's driving me crazy," Nanny said. "I can't think straight. Yesterday in chemistry, Mr. Trapezi asked me what a heavy metal was, and I said I heard that Cured Meats was an awesome band."

Lisa nodded. She'd been pretty preoccupied herself. Yesterday, she'd gone through the entire morning without realizing she was wearing one pink sock and one yellow sock. Everyone at school had thought she was starting a new fashion trend. She'd spotted a couple of sophomores in different-colored socks this morning. While she was glad of the proof that she was a Bayside fashion leader, she wasn't crazy about the reminder that her brain was fried.

"That's why I've come up with a new plan," Nanny continued. "I've got to find out once and for all if I have a chance with Cal. I want you to talk to him, Lisa."

"*Me?*" Lisa said. "Gosh, Nanny. I don't know."

"You're the perfect person," Nanny insisted. "You can find out if Cal is going to the masquerade ball. Ask him if he has a date. Whatever you do, don't mention my name, though. I don't want to be completely humiliated. Just hint a lot. That way, if he's not interested, I can always say you were talking about someone else. Will you do it, Lisa?"

Lisa put the lipstick back in her purse and pretended to search for her blush. She was stalling and she knew it. She wasn't crazy about talking to Cal on Nanny's behalf. But Nanny was looking at her with those big brown calf eyes of hers. And their project for Ms. McCracken *was* on courtship. She couldn't back down now.

"Okay," she told Nanny. "I'll do it."

▲   ▼   ▲

Jessie slipped into the costume Kelly had made. Kelly had dropped it off on the way to school, and Mrs. Spano had left it on Jessie's bed while Jessie was in the shower.

She lifted the shimmering green gossamer out of the box. Kelly had done an awesome job, Jessie had to admit. The top was spring green velvet with dangling glass beads. The pants were wide and gauzy.

Jessie looked at the clock. She knew she was going to be late for her first class, but she couldn't resist trying it on. It would only take a minute.

She wiggled out of her jeans and T-shirt and slipped on the cropped velvet top and the gauzy pants. Then she quickly ran over to the full-length mirror.

Jessie gasped in delight. It was perfect! She'd add bracelets and long, dangling earrings. Slater would completely freak when he saw her!

Jessie began to twirl in front of the mirror in delight. She loved the way the material moved. Under the lights at the country club, the glass beads would shimmer. She twirled faster and faster, imagining herself at the country club with everyone watching her admiringly. Especially one pair of soft brown eyes.

Suddenly, Jessie noticed a piece of gossamer material fly off. It drifted slowly down to the floor. As she twirled, other pieces of material began to fly off. The seam on the outside of her pants separated. Another piece of material flapped and then flew off.

In just another moment, Jessie was standing in front of the mirror in her underwear.

"Kelly Kapowski, you're dead meat!" she shrieked.

Chapter 10

▲ ▼ ▲ ▼ ▲

In the gym locker room, Kelly bent over to lace up her sneakers. The last thing she felt like doing right now was bouncing around playing volleyball. But somehow she didn't think Coach Turk would consider having a good cry an aerobic activity.

She pulled her Bayside High sweatshirt on over her head. When her face emerged, she was hit in the face with something soft. Kelly saw something green drift down to the locker room floor.

She blinked, surprised. Jessie was standing in front of her, clutching the green material of her costume. Only it wasn't her costume. It was just . . . material.

"Jessie?" Kelly asked, confused. "Where's your costume?"

"Here," Jessie said, shaking fistfuls of the material in front of Kelly's face. A piece of material drifted down past her nose. "And here." Jessie began to pluck pieces of the material out of her hands. She threw them into the air. "And here. And here, and here, and here, and—"

"Jessie, what happened?" Kelly asked, shocked.

"You know very well what happened!" Jessie yelled. "You deliberately made my costume so it would fall apart! As soon as I'd start dancing, the costume would break down. I'd be standing there in my underwear!"

Across the locker room, Cissy Garlock made a thumbs-up signal. "Score one for you, Kapowski," she called. Everyone in the senior class knew about Kelly and Jessie's feud.

Jean-Marie Howell giggled. "You would have been awfully popular, Jessie."

"Do you *mind*?" Jessie said, annoyed.

"Jessie, I didn't do it on purpose," Kelly said earnestly. "I promise."

"You expect me to believe that?" Jessie asked scornfully. "You were getting back at me for turning your hair green! You were spiteful and cruel and . . . spiteful!"

"Jessie, I swear I didn't!" Kelly said. "I was just following Nanny's pattern." But she had been distracted, Kelly thought worriedly. She'd been thinking about Zack.

"Aha!" Jessie cried. "I see it in your face. Guilt!

You did do it!"

"I didn't!" Kelly protested. "Jessie, I'll do it over again tonight. It will be as good as new. I promise."

Kelly bent down to pick up the material, but Jessie snatched it away from her fingers. "No way," Jessie said. "Fool me once, shame on you. Fool me twice, shame on me. I'm not going to let you touch this costume. I'll make a different one."

"But, Jessie, you can't sew," Kelly pointed out.

"I'll do it somehow. If I have to stay up all night, I'll figure it out," Jessie said. "Because I'll never trust you again, Kelly Kapowski! And I'll never, *ever* forgive you!"

▲　▼　▲

Lisa had once memorized Cal's schedule when she'd had a crush on him, and she knew he had a free period when she did. She also knew he went to the library.

When she'd been interested in him, she'd gone to the library during her free period instead of to the cafeteria to gossip. She'd arranged herself in his line of sight and opened her books. He'd never looked up, and she had never made any headway. But her grades had really improved.

Today, she discovered Cal sitting on a window seat. He was bent over a book of short stories. Lisa sat down beside him.

"Hi," she whispered.

Cal looked up. "Hi, Lisa. How's it going?"

"Okay," Lisa said. It was a small window seat, so she was sitting very close to him. She hadn't been this close to Cal since they'd dated. She'd forgotten he had one dimple in his left cheek that made his grin lopsided. Lisa was glad she was sitting down. All of a sudden, she felt a little weak in the knees.

"Lisa? Is there a problem?"

Lisa gripped her books in her lap. She could feel her palms begin to perspire as she realized she hadn't prepared what she was going to say. "No problem," she said brightly.

"Shhhhh," Ms. Grinko, the librarian, warned.

"No problem," Lisa repeated in a whisper. "Actually, I have some good news for you. Someone has a crush on you, but she's really shy."

Cal frowned. "Someone?"

"Well, I can't say who it is," Lisa said. "I'm sworn to secrecy. I'll give you a few hints, though. Hmmmm . . . It's someone you'd never expect. Someone you've spent a lot of time with. When you see her, you think newspaper. And she was at the Bring-Your-Old-Boyfriend Barbecue."

Cal looked uncomfortable. He was blushing, Lisa saw. He gazed downward, not meeting her eyes. "I see," he said slowly.

"Is that all you can say?" Lisa murmured, leaning closer. "Are you interested or not? What should I tell her?"

Cal leaned back. "I don't know about this, Lisa. I

mean, it's really flattering. But I don't like all this . . . undercover stuff."

"So you *are* interested?" Lisa persisted. "Do you have a date for the ball tomorrow night?"

Cal stood up. "Look, Lisa. I'm interested, sure. And I'm going stag to the ball. But I don't want to talk about this here. I—I'll just talk to her at the ball. I have to go." He turned and hurried out of the library.

Lisa frowned. Cal had seemed so uncomfortable. Maybe he didn't like having an ex-girlfriend as a go-between. He'd really seemed embarrassed and shy. That wasn't like Cal.

Lisa looked down at her hands and groaned. The school paper had been on top of her books, and thanks to her perspiring palms, she now had newsprint all over her hands. She got up to head for the girls' room.

Suddenly, Lisa stopped, frozen. "When you see her, you think newspaper," she had said.

She'd been holding a newspaper! That's why Cal had looked down that way.

She was someone he'd spent a lot of time with. She was someone who'd been at the barbecue. And she was certainly someone he'd never expect.

Cal thought she'd been talking about herself!

That's why he'd been so embarrassed. That's why he'd left so quickly. He'd been too flustered and surprised to respond.

Lisa thought back over Cal's reaction. He had

been flustered, no question. But he'd also been *pleased*. And how did she feel?

Lisa sat back down, dazed. She examined her feelings and discovered that she didn't feel embarrassed. She felt relieved!

She could finally admit to herself that the reason she'd been feeling uncomfortable helping Nanny snare Cal was that she wanted him for herself. She *did* still have a crush on him. He was the nicest, most fun boy she'd ever dated and she had just let him go without a second thought. She had imagined that another boy just like him was right around the corner.

And another boy had been around the corner. Jeff Racine. But no matter how much Lisa liked Jeff, and she liked him a lot, she didn't feel quite the same way about him. There was just an extra *ping* when it came to her feelings for Cal. Or maybe it was a *zing*. Whatever it was, Lisa wanted it back.

And this time, she wasn't going to bow out gracefully. She wasn't going to hand Nanny to him on a silver platter. She didn't want to hurt Nanny, but she didn't want to lose Cal again, either.

No more games, Lisa thought determinedly. On Saturday night, she and Cal would have a talk. She'd tell him exactly how she felt.

▲ ▼ ▲

Friday night, Kelly sat in her bedroom, brooding. She and Slater had decided not to get together. She had told him that she had tons of studying to do, but it wasn't true. She just hadn't wanted to see him. The funny thing was, she had the feeling that Slater was avoiding her, too.

Maybe it didn't have anything to do with Slater, Kelly reasoned. She hadn't wanted to see anyone else, either. She'd turned down watching TV with her parents and a cutthroat game of Monopoly with her brothers Kirby and Kerry. She'd even turned down a shopping trip to the mall with her younger sister, Nicki. She had just wanted to be alone.

But now that she was alone, she didn't know what to do with herself. Kelly looked around the room. She should do something constructive, she decided. That would make her feel better. Maybe she could give her room a good spring cleaning. Her mother would be so happy, she'd turn a couple of million cartwheels to celebrate.

Kelly moved to the desk. She hadn't cleaned it out in ages. The big bottom drawer was full of junk. She tossed everything in there that she didn't know what else to do with, like photographs and old invitations and report cards.

Kelly opened the drawer. Her aunt had given her a photograph album for Christmas. Maybe a good project would be to take her favorite photos and put them in the book. She reached into the drawer and took out a handful.

Jessie's face smiled up at her. They were at the beach, and Jessie was wearing this silly straw hat her mother had brought back from Hawaii. It had palm trees and pineapples on it. Kelly grinned, remembering.

She leafed through the photos. Here was Jessie on her sixteenth birthday. She was wearing the blue silk blouse Lisa and Kelly had chipped in to buy her. All three of them had gone to this swanky downtown restaurant, Adolfo's, for lunch. They hadn't had enough cash to pay the bill so Kelly and Jessie had ordered coffee while Lisa had driven home to borrow money from her mom. But Lisa had hit a sale on the way back and then had had to go home again to get more cash. By the time she'd showed up, Jessie and Kelly were so full of coffee they didn't get a wink of sleep all night.

Kelly laughed out loud. She pulled out a photograph of her and Jessie at twelve. Jessie looked skinny and gawky. That was the year she'd shot up to her present height. Kelly had braces on her teeth. They were giggling about something in the picture. They were always laughing about something.

Kelly sighed as she sifted through more photos. Jessie was in most of them. First grade, wearing a plaid dress. Fifth grade, holding a softball mitt. Seventh grade, trying out for basketball, with Kelly standing by in her first cheerleader's uniform.

Kelly's eyes filled with tears. She'd known Jessie for so long! They'd had a million fights and made up a million times. What made this fight so bitter that they couldn't even talk to each other?

Boys.

That's what made the difference, Kelly thought sorrowfully. Guys messed up everything. Suddenly, when your whole heart was involved, things got serious.

But my whole heart isn't involved, Kelly thought suddenly. *Not with Slater. And Jessie's is.*

Kelly put down the photograph she was holding. She could scarcely breathe. For the first time in weeks, everything was clear.

She didn't want Slater. She liked him, she enjoyed his company, and he was a wonderful guy to date. But her best friend loved him, and she'd never feel comfortable going out with him. No matter what.

She and Jessie couldn't break up over a guy, Kelly thought. Especially a guy Kelly wasn't sure she wanted!

But Jessie thought Kelly had sabotaged that costume on purpose. She said she'd never forgive her. How could Kelly prove her innocence? How could she show Jessie that she was sincere?

▲　▼　▲

Jessie flopped back on her bed with a groan. She didn't know why she was depressed. Everything was going her way. Her mother had taken all the material and had told Jessie not to worry. She didn't have to think of another costume. Mrs. Spano would revive her old sewing skills and fix that one. She'd even found some great silver bangles for Jessie to wear on her wrists.

Zack had called earlier and told her that he'd heard Slater and Kelly weren't going out tonight, so would Jessie mind if they didn't go out on a date? Nobody would see them, anyway. And tomorrow night, they'd flaunt their love in Slater and Kelly's face at the ball. Jessie had been happy to stay home. She was exhausted.

And depressed. "But why?" Jessie wondered aloud.

Jessie sat up determinedly. Enough negative vibes. She was tired of feeling confused. She had things to do. First of all, she had to find the mask she planned to wear tomorrow night. She'd bought one for a Mardi Gras party she'd gone to junior year. It had to be somewhere.

Jessie stood on tiptoe to reach the shelf at the top of her closet. There was a box up there filled with letters and party favors and all kinds of junk. She was pretty sure that the mask was in there.

She pulled the box forward with her fingertips. It tipped, and she lost her grip. The box tumbled onto the floor, spilling out its contents.

"Great," Jessie grumbled. The mask had fallen, and she picked it up. It was black satin with peacock feathers. Jessie smoothed the feathers. It looked as cool as the day she and Kelly had found it. They'd both loved it so much that they'd bought the same one.

Jessie tossed the mask up on the bed and knelt to gather the letters and cards that had spilled onto the carpet. She recognized Kelly's round handwriting on an envelope. The girl could never write in a straight line, Jessie thought, smiling faintly.

She picked up a postcard Kelly had written to her from a trip her family had taken to Vancouver. There was just one word on it: *Help!* Jessie laughed out loud.

She scooped up all the letters Kelly had written her from camp when she was ten years old.

The invitation to Kelly's sweet sixteen party. The notes they'd exchanged on that sleepy afternoon in geography class in eighth grade. They'd both gotten Saturday detention for three whole weeks. Somehow, they'd even had fun there.

Jessie sighed, the letters in her lap. She and Kelly had been through thick and thin together. Braces and first crushes and her parents' divorce. She must be crazy to think she could just cut Kelly out of her life. Even for a guy's sake.

Especially for a guy's sake. No matter how much she loved Slater, it wasn't worth it.

But how could she show Kelly that she'd had a change of heart? Kelly wasn't talking to her right now. And there was probably no chance of a normal dialogue until Kelly's hair returned to normal. How could Jessie get Kelly to believe that she'd never do such an awful thing to her very best friend?

Chapter 11

▲ ▼ ▲ ▼ ▲

The Fool Moon Madness Masquerade Ball was an annual event at the Half Moon Country Club. The club went all out, twining tiny white lights around the tree trunks and branches, decorating the elegant patio with masses of white flowers, and lighting what seemed to be a hundred golden candles.

A band was playing soft music in the elegant ballroom, but the guests were free to wander around the country club grounds. The full moon and starry sky caused the outdoors to be almost as bright as inside the club.

Kelly walked into the club arm in arm with Slater. She was wearing a mask she'd bought for a Mardi Gras party last year. She'd thought she'd feel like a complete goon in a mask, but now that she was at the ball, she liked it. She liked being able to mingle without anyone knowing who she was.

Slater looked almost sinister in the black mask, black suit, and black shirt he was wearing. He had decided to come to the ball as Zorro, since he didn't have to buy anything new except a hat. He'd said it was the best costume he could come up with without money or an imagination.

Kelly slipped out of her trench coat and handed it to the coat check.

Slater gave a low whistle. "You know, I never thought I'd say this, momma, but your green hair looks cool. Especially with that outfit."

"Thanks," Kelly said. "Can I meet you inside?"

"Look for me by the snacks," Slater advised.

Kelly hurried toward the ladies' room. On the way inside, she almost bumped into a full-length mirror. Then she realized it was Jessie.

"Jessie!"

"Kelly!"

Kelly peered at her through her mask. "What are you doing with green hair?"

"I dyed it green to prove to you that I didn't do yours deliberately," Jessie admitted. "I thought you might feel better if you weren't the only one with green hair. What are you doing in my costume?"

"I wanted to prove to you that I followed Nanny's pattern," Kelly said. "So I made it all over again, the exact same way."

Jessie gasped. "But, Kelly—"

Kelly leaned closer. "Don't worry. I'm wearing a body stocking underneath."

Just then, Lisa and Nanny came in. They both did a double take when they saw Kelly and Jessie.

Lisa circled them slowly, her eyes glinting behind her Catwoman mask. "It's incredible," she said. "If Jessie wasn't so tall, I wouldn't be able to tell you guys apart. But can I ask you something, Jessie? Why is your hair green?"

Jessie laughed and explained. "So I went and bought the book," she said, "and I saw that the instructions for a different rinse were on a facing page from the one we'd wanted. It said to never use it on brown hair, so I tried it. It came out perfectly."

"I guess," Lisa said. "If you enjoy looking like you have seaweed for hair. Gosh, Kelly, I'm so sorry. That was pretty stupid."

"I think it was super of Jessie," Kelly said warmly. "I'll never forget it."

"I bet I messed up, too," Nanny said mournfully. "I'm sure I left a step out of that pattern. Did I mention reinforcing the seams?"

Kelly shook her head.

Nanny sighed. "It's all Cal's fault. I've got him on the brain."

Me, too, Lisa almost said.

"Well, it's all over now," Jessie said. "I'm just glad I have my best friend back."

"Me, too," Kelly said.

"Whatever happens with the guys in our lives, we'll always be friends," Jessie said, and the two girls hugged.

▲   ▼   ▲

Slater cruised the snacks, but he really wasn't hungry. The band was playing a great number, but he didn't feel like dancing. He hadn't felt like himself all week.

No, longer than that, Slater thought with a grimace. If he had to be honest, he'd have to say he hadn't felt right since he'd started to date Kelly. He'd felt off-balance and just plain weird. Sometimes, he wasn't even hungry! Last night, he'd refused second helpings of his mother's meat loaf. She'd felt his forehead and asked him if he had a temperature.

It wasn't that he didn't like Kelly—he did. Who wouldn't? He'd enjoyed every second of their dates and always looked forward to seeing her smiling face the next time.

It was his other friendships that were all messed up. The gang just wasn't the same anymore, and he missed that. Maybe he hadn't realized how important all his friends were to him. He'd tended to focus on girlfriend problems. He hadn't realized that having friend problems could be just as big a drag.

He'd been avoiding Kelly this week, and he was sure she knew it. Maybe she even felt the same way.

Slater roamed out onto the patio. To his surprise,

he saw Kelly sitting under the shadow of a tree. He walked over to her and sat down.

"I'm glad you're out here," he said. "I really wanted to talk to you in private, Kelly."

He saw her give a start. She probably knew what was coming.

"Look, we've been avoiding each other this week," he said. "And I think I know why. It's not working, Kelly. We can't exist in a vacuum. We can't have fun when we know our friends are miserable. I can't stand seeing Jessie so unhappy and knowing that I'm the cause of it." Slater sighed. "I don't know if Jessie and I are meant to be. Everything I told you about us is true. Our relationship was full of ups and downs. I never knew what was going on. And being with you is just . . . easy. And fun. But—"

Slater waited hopefully for Kelly to say something. It wasn't like her to let him struggle on this way. Usually, she'd say the right thing to make him feel better. But maybe she was trying not to cry.

"I'm not saying I want to get back with Jessie," Slater said. "And I don't know if you really belong with Zack. But maybe we owe it to them to try to figure out why we just can't let go. Kelly, I think it would be better for everybody if we broke up."

Behind the mask, Jessie listened to Slater silently. She hadn't meant to impersonate Kelly. But once he'd confused them, she hadn't been able to resist hearing what he had to say.

At first, she'd been overjoyed to hear that Slater wanted to break up with Kelly. She'd hardly been able to hear his words over the beating of her heart. But slowly his words had sunk in.

He was so *sad,* Jessie thought. Loving her wasn't easy. It was almost like he loved her against his better judgment.

"Do you want to go inside?" Slater asked.

Jessie shook her head.

"Should I—leave you alone?" he said gently.

Jessie nodded. A tear slipped down her cheek as Slater walked back into the party. For the first time, it occurred to Jessie that Slater could have been right all along. No matter how much they loved each other, maybe they just weren't meant to be.

▲ ▼ ▲

Zack looked for Jessie everywhere. He finally found her sitting on a windowsill in the hallway. The hall was lit with candles, and he could barely make out her features in the gloom.

"Jessie, I've been looking for you," he said. He tugged uncomfortably at his costume. Weeks ago, he'd decided to come to the ball dressed as a devil. Now here he was in a shiny red suit, with horns and a pitchfork. He hadn't realized how appropriate the costume would be.

Zack noticed Jessie flinch, but she didn't turn. She just kept looking out the window.

"I know you're mad at me," Zack said. "You have

every right to be. I did promise you that I'd hold to our bargain. But, Jessie, I can't keep pretending that we're dating. I can't lie to Kelly that way. I have too much respect for her. I have to tell her the truth. Is that okay?"

Behind the mask, Kelly heard Zack's words and her heart sang. He wasn't involved with Jessie! A soft sigh escaped her, but Zack didn't hear it. Kelly reached up to take off the mask and show him who she was.

"And then there's Irina," Zack said.

Kelly stopped.

"I know you were mad when I kept taking her out instead of you," Zack said. "I had to for Screech's sake, but I'll explain about that later. The point is, something happened. Last night, we went to the beach and talked and talked. I think I'm falling in love with her."

Kelly gasped.

"Jessie? I didn't mean to hurt you—"

Kelly sprang to her feet. She jumped off the windowsill and whirled around to run away. A bit of gossamer material floated off her costume.

"Jessie?" Zack asked, puzzled.

Kelly started to run. Bits of her costume flew off as she dashed down the hallway. The last things to hit the floor were the panels of her gauzy trousers.

"Kelly!" Zack breathed.

Chapter 12

▲ ▼ ▲ ▼ ▲

Zack wandered all over the grounds looking for Kelly. Everywhere he went he saw angels and mermaids and tigers. He saw three Scarlett O'Haras and four Captain Kirks and three Catwomen. One of them was Lisa, who told him she hadn't seen Kelly or Jessie in a while.

Zack found Slater morosely watching a moonlit game of tennis. The match was being played by the Beast from *Beauty and the Beast* and a woman wearing a top hat and tails.

"Hey, Slater," he called as he came up. "Have you seen Kelly?"

Slater looked at him, startled. Zack guessed that he hadn't asked Slater a direct question in a couple of weeks. In fact, he'd barely talked to him.

"No," he said. "Not since I talked to her on the

patio. I left her sitting there alone for awhile. She wasn't, um, in the mood to talk."

Zack eyed him. "Are you sure it was Kelly?"

Slater looked at him, puzzled. "What do you mean? Of course it was Kelly. How could I miss that green hair?"

Zack groaned. "Have I got a story for you." Quickly, Zack filled him in on Kelly and Jessie's look-alike costumes and his talk with "Jessie."

"I'm not sure what's up," Zack said. "I *do* know that Jessie put a green rinse in her hair to prove to Kelly that she didn't ruin hers deliberately."

"And Kelly said she was wearing Jessie's costume to prove the same thing," Slater said. He hit his forehead. "That means that I probably told Jessie that I wanted to break up with Kelly."

"You broke up with Kelly?" Zack said, startled. "You slime!"

"I thought you didn't want me to date her!" Slater barked.

"I don't! But how could you break up with her?" Zack demanded. "She's perfect!"

"I know," Slater said. "But she's not perfect for me. And I'm not perfect for her."

Zack frowned, concerned. "How did she take it?"

"I don't know," Slater said. "She might have been Jessie, remember? She probably was Jessie. She did seem kind of tall. I remember thinking she was probably wearing heels."

"I thought you said she was sitting down," Zack said.

"I did," Slater said sheepishly. "I was nervous, man. What can I say? I wasn't thinking straight. But why didn't Jessie say something? Why didn't Kelly say something to you?"

Zack sighed. "Who knows? Maybe because for once they were hearing the truth. None of us has been straight with each other lately. Or maybe we haven't been straight with ourselves."

Slater nodded. "That's for sure."

There was an awkward pause.

"Look—" Zack started.

"Listen—" Slater said.

They grinned at each other.

"Friends?" Zack said. "No matter what happens with Jessie and Kelly? Assuming we can tell them apart, that is."

"Friends," Slater said.

Just then, the guys saw two girls with green hair heading toward them. Kelly was now wearing her trench coat over her body stocking.

"What do you know," Zack said. "At last we can tell you guys apart."

"Zack and I figured out that we made our confessions to the wrong girls," Slater said sourly.

"We're sorry, guys," Jessie said. "We didn't mean to fool you that way."

"I ran into Jessie in the ladies' room," Kelly said

to Zack. "I told her what you thought you told her."

"And I told Kelly what you thought you told her," Jessie said to Slater. "You were very sweet."

Slater looked at Kelly. "Is everything okay?"

Kelly nodded. "Everything's fine. You were right, Slater. I was thinking the very same thing. I'm just glad we're all friends again. We are, aren't we?"

Zack and Slater nodded. "You bet."

Jessie summoned up a smile. She wasn't happy about Slater. But she was happy she had her friends back. That made all the difference.

"Kelly," Zack said in a low tone, "what I said about Irina—"

Kelly slipped her mask back on. "Forget it, Zack. It doesn't matter. I understand."

Lisa hurried up to them, her tail twitching. "Has anyone seen Cal? I know he'll be wearing an owl mask. Nanny told me. Has anyone seen an owl?"

"Who?" Zack asked.

"Who?" Kelly said.

"Exactly!" Lisa said triumphantly.

▲   ▼   ▲

Cal Everhart stepped into the entrance of the country club. He saw Jeff Racine, a tennis buddy, poke his head into the hall. Then Jeff caught sight of Cal.

"Have you see Lisa?" Jeff asked.

Cal slipped his feathered owl mask over his head. "I just got here."

"Great mask," Jeff said.

"Actually, it's kind of tight," Cal said. "I tried to wear it on the way over here just to impress the other drivers on the road. But it's really uncomfortable. Do you think my nose is too big? Hey, don't answer that."

"Well, it looks great," Jeff said, grinning. "Lisa would say that's what's really important."

"Lisa is used to heels and electric curlers," Cal said, slipping off the mask with a grimace. "She's had more training in pain than I have."

Jeff laughed. "Here," he said, handing Cal his parrot mask. "We can trade if you like."

Cal slipped the mask on. "Ahhh," he said in relief. "That's much better. Point me toward the birdseed, will you? And if I see Lisa, I'll give you a squawk."

▲   ▼   ▲

A few minutes later, Lisa scooted out into the hall and almost ran into Cal.

"There you are!" he said. She could barely hear him behind the owl mask. But to her surprise, he swept her up into a hug.

Lisa's cheeks glowed. Cal did have a crush on her! She was right!

Lisa had been waiting so long to talk to him that the words spilled out of her in a rush. "Oh, Cal," she murmured. "I'm so glad you just did that. I feel the same way. The other day in the library, I was so glad when I realized you suspected that I was the one who had a crush on you. You saw my secret. That must mean it was meant to be. I want to get back together. Do you, Cal?"

Slowly, Cal reached up and removed the mask. Lisa gasped in horror. It wasn't Cal at all. It was Jeff Racine!

"Jeff!" she cried. "It's you!"

"Sorry to disappoint you," Jeff said icily.

"I—I—" Lisa stammered.

"It's okay, Lisa," Jeff said. "I don't think there's anything you can say right now that I want to hear." He turned around and stalked off.

Lisa started after Jeff, but she was stopped by a shrill scream. She hurried to the door of the ballroom. Through the crowd, she saw Irina Pastovic, her face white, weave as though she would fall. Her jeweled mask fell to the floor at her feet and Nanny picked it up. Irina put her hands to her face.

"What's wrong?" Lisa asked aloud.

Alan Zobel was standing next to her. "It must be what happened in Zoldavia today," he said.

"What happened?" Lisa asked.

"The cease-fire collapsed," Alan told her. "I heard it on the radio on the way here. Karkasha was shelled today. A whole neighorhood of the city was destroyed."

"Oh, my gosh," Lisa said. "Poor Irina."

Suddenly, Irina began to push her way through the crowd. She hurried to the door of the patio, slipped through it, and disappeared.

"Her parents are still in Karkasha, right?" Alan asked.

"Yes," Lisa said numbly.

"It makes our problems seem small, doesn't it?" Alan asked.

Lisa stared out at the cold moon. "Yes, it does," she said softly.

▲ ▼ ▲

Zack heard the news a few minutes later. He was standing outside talking to a group of Bayside kids when Jennifer Ralston mentioned Irina's cry and her sudden disappearance.

"When did it happen?" he asked, instantly concerned.

"A few minutes ago," Jennifer said. "Nobody knows where Irina disappeared to. Nanny said she doesn't have a car."

Zack hurried away from the group. He had to find Irina. He should be the one to comfort her. Until they got more news, she wouldn't have any information about her parents and their safety. It would be a long night, and Zack wanted to be with her.

When Zack dashed into the ballroom, he spotted Screech across the floor. Screech was dressed as a pirate in a striped T-shirt and a satin eye patch. Zack pushed through the crowd toward him.

"What ho, me hearty!" Screech greeted him, brandishing a plastic sword.

"Have you heard?" Zack asked. "Karkasha was

shelled today. Irina heard the news and practically fainted. Doesn't that prove she can't be a spy?"

"Where is she now?" Screech asked.

"I don't know," Zack said, running a hand through his hair. "I have to find her, Screech."

"There's the gang," Screech said. "Let's ask them if they've seen her."

Screech and Zack hurried toward the group. "Has anyone seen Irina?" Screech asked.

Jessie shook her head. "Did you hear about the cease-fire violation?"

Zack nodded. "Jennifer said Irina almost fainted."

Lisa nodded. "I saw it. It was awful."

"I've got to find her!" Zack said.

Kelly looked away. She swallowed against a lump in her throat. *Zack is frantic,* she thought. *He really must be in love.*

Then Kelly took a deep breath. She had no right to be hurt. She had to be glad for him. Irina was a good person who was all alone in this country. She needed someone like Zack.

Nanny rushed up to them, her face streaked with tears. Her red wig was askew, and her mascara was running. "Oh, Lisa!" she cried. "How could this have happened!"

Lisa started guiltily. "Gosh," she said. "How did you find out? Nanny, I don't know what to say. Sometimes life just whacks you upside the head. You

think you know who you're in love with, and—
wham— it turns out to be somebody else."

"You're telling me," Kelly muttered.

"Irina dropped her mask and I picked it up,"
Nanny burbled. She twisted the material of her gold
dress, and some sequins dropped off. "It's so pretty,
with all those jewels on it. She bought it in Paris. So I
put it on and kept on looking for Cal. I found him!"
Nanny burst into fresh tears.

Lisa began to see that she just might be off the
hook. Maybe Nanny wasn't talking about her crush
on Cal. "What happened?" she asked. "And stop
twisting that dress, girl. There's no reason to ruin a
perfectly good fashion statement."

"He thought I was Irina," Nanny said between
sobs. "He was all upset. He told me—I mean Irina—
that they had to switch to the emergency plan. He
said he'd meet me—Irina—in the parking lot."
Nanny swiped at her cheeks. "He was involved with
Irina all along," she said. "They've been carrying on
behind everyone's back. How could I have been so
stupid?"

Lisa put her arm around Nanny. "Now, now," she
soothed. "You don't know anything for sure."

Zack motioned to Screech and drew him a few
paces away. "Are you thinking what I'm thinking?"

Screech nodded, his eyes on Nanny. "That
Nanny looks pretty even when she cries?" he asked
dreamily.

Zack punched Screech on the shoulder. "That Cal Everhart is in cahoots with Irina!"

Screech gasped. "You mean they're *both* spies?"

"I don't know, Screech," Zack said. "But something's fishy. Why did he say they needed to follow the emergency plan? And why the secret meeting in the parking lot?" He snapped his fingers. "Wait a second. Didn't Cal say at the party that he has a Zoldavian grandmother?"

"Oh, my gosh!" Screech shrieked. "They are spies! I knew I should have worn my James Bond costume!"

"I bet I know where Cal and Irina are going," Zack said.

Suddenly, Zack and Screech found themselves surrounded. But it wasn't by counterintelligence agents. It was by Jessie, Slater, Lisa, and Kelly.

"What's going on?" Jessie asked.

"Who's a spy?" Slater demanded.

"What does this have to do with Irina?" Kelly asked.

"And Cal?" Lisa added.

Zack and Screech exchanged glances. "It's a long story," Zack said.

"And we have to get to the government plant," Screech said. "Zack, let's synchronize our watches."

"Screech, we're going together," Zack said patiently. "We don't have to do that."

"What are you guys talking about?" Jessie asked,

frustrated.

"Are you in trouble?" Slater asked.

"Tell us so we can help," Kelly said.

Zack looked at his watch. "Like I said, it's a long story," he said. "We'll tell you on the way."

Chapter 13

▲ ▼ ▲ ▼ ▲

Zack was only a block away from the plant when he smacked his head with his hand. "I just thought of something," he said to the gang. "How are we going to get inside after hours?"

Screech reached into the pocket of his striped T-shirt. He waved an ID in the air. "Press pass," he said gleefully.

"Good work, Screech," Zack told him.

"If I break this story, I can win Nanny back," Screech said. "I came prepared for anything."

They pulled up to the building. The gate was closed, and a guard was standing in front of it. He walked over to the driver's side.

"Can I help you folks?" he asked.

Screech leaned over and flashed his press pass. "We're from the Palisades *Gazette,*" he said. "We're doing team coverage tonight on the employees who work here after hours."

The guard slowly moved his gaze over Screech's pirate outfit and Zack's devil costume. Then he squinted into the backseat at a genie, Catwoman, Zorro, and a girl in a trench coat with green hair.

Zack spoke up quickly. "We were just covering another story," he said. "The masquerade ball at the country club."

"For the society pages," Lisa piped up.

"The press never rests," Slater offered. Kelly just gave the guard a friendly smile.

The guard tossed the pass back into Screech's lap. "Why do I always pull duty on the night of a full moon?" he asked, rolling his eyes. "Go ahead, folks."

Zack put the Mustang in gear, and they drove through the gates. He parked in a dark corner of the parking lot. Then he and Screech quickly and stealthily led the way to where they'd seen Irina signal the third-floor office.

"She's not there," Screech whispered, disappointed.

"Look," Zack murmured. He pointed above. The light in the office was on. "I bet they're up there right now," he said.

A shadow crossed the window. "That was Cal!" Lisa whispered. "I'd know that gorgeous profile anywhere."

"We have to get inside," Zack said. "Maybe we

can hear something through the office wall next door."

"Follow me," Screech said.

The gang quickly ran up to the building entrance. The door was open, but the interior glass doors were locked.

"No problem," Screech said. "I watched Barney the last time he punched in his code. I remembered the numbers because they were the same as my grandmother's birthday."

Screech punched in 4-2-7. Suddenly, a red light began to blink. Letters flashed across the screen of the keypad. WRONG CODE. YOU HAVE FIVE SECONDS TO RETRY.

"Screech, it's the wrong number!" Zack said frantically. "What happened?"

"I could have sworn it was my grandmother's birthday," Screech fretted. "I remember because last May twenty-seventh, I forgot to send her a card—"

"May isn't *four*, Screech!" Jessie exclaimed. "It's five!"

"Oh," Screech said. "I always get that mixed up."

"Punch it in!" Zack yelled.

Quickly, Screech punched in 5-2-7. The red light changed to green, and Zack tried the door. It opened.

"Whew," he said. "That was close."

When they got to the keypad for the stairwell, Screech punched in the same number. The door clicked open.

"No wonder I never remember her birthday," he muttered.

They tiptoed up the stairs, listening for any sound. But the building was dim and empty. The fluorescent lights flickered eerily.

At the third floor, Zack put a finger to his lips. He opened the door slowly and looked out. The hallway was empty.

"Come on," he whispered.

The rest of the gang piled out behind him and moved as quietly as they could down the hall. They noticed a thin stream of light coming from underneath the door of the third office.

"Let's try the office next door first," Zack whispered. "Then we can—"

But he was drowned out by a loud *pop*.

"What was that?" Kelly asked nervously.

"It sounded like a car backfiring," Slater said.

Jessie swallowed. "Don't they say that a car backfiring sounds like a . . . a gunshot?"

"Oh, no!" Zack cried. "Irina!"

The gang charged down the hall. Slater got to the door first. He reached for the knob.

"It's locked," he said frantically.

"Let's break it down!" Zack gasped.

Together, Zack and Slater slammed their shoulders against the door. They heard it splinter, and after another heave, it crashed open. Zack and Slater practically fell into the office with the rest of the gang on their heels.

Mark Quigley was holding a foaming bottle of sparkling cider. Cal and Irina were holding out glasses. They all wore the same stunned expression.

"Aha!" Screech said, extricating himself from Lisa's tail. "We caught you red-handed!"

"With what?" Cal said. "Cider? Are you the fermented apple patrol?"

Mark Quigley blinked at Screech. "Don't I know you?"

Screech adjusted his eye patch. "Aha! You see through my disguise with the dastardly eye of a master *spy*!"

"If you ask me, you're the one with the weird eye, Screech," Cal said with a nod at the satin eye patch.

"What is going on?" Irina asked. "I'm confused. Who is a spy?"

"You are!" Screech thundered, pointing to Cal and Irina.

"Me?" Irina asked.

Cal laughed. "*Me?* Only in my dreams."

Zack stepped forward. "Irina, why don't you tell us what's going on. Why are you here?"

"Mark is helping me," Irina said. "Karkasha was bombed today."

"We heard," Kelly said gently. "We're really sorry."

"I coordinate the surveillance of the area for the government," Mark explained. "I get up-to-the-minute details of which area has been shelled, block by block and house by house."

"Mark is my brother-in-law," Cal explained. "When I met Irina, I told her that he might be able to help her."

"I cleared it with my supervisor," Mark went on, pouring the cider into Irina's glass. "I'm allowed to give unclassified information to Irina, since she's a Zoldavian who still has family members back home. That way, she can keep up with what's going on at home more accurately than she can through the newspapers or TV." He smiled at Irina. "Our government is glad to help out. Her parents are very active in the peace movement in Zoldavia."

"That's why we're celebrating tonight," Cal said, holding out his glass so Mark could fill it. "We found out that Irina's parents are safe. Their neighborhood was untouched."

"I was so relieved," Irina said. "Thanks to Mark. And Cal."

Cal held up his glass. "To your parents."

Irina held up her glass. "To my parents. And to you," she added softly.

Lisa gulped. Maybe Nanny had been right. There *was* something between Irina and Cal. There was enough electricity in this room to light all of Palisades.

"Wait a second," Screech said. "Why all the secret signaling? Why did you have to throw the information to Irina that way?"

"Simple," Mark said. "Irina has a bad hip, and the elevator is out. Plus, I'm lazy. We just devised a system to make it easier on both of us."

"What's the emergency plan?" Zack asked Cal.

Cal tore his gaze away from Irina. "In case something happened in Zoldavia while Mark wasn't at work, we could page him. That's all it meant. How do you know about that?"

"Never mind," Zack said with a sigh.

Cal stepped over to Lisa and pulled her aside.

"I've got to thank you," he murmured. "If it wasn't for you, I never would have gotten the courage to tell Irina how I felt."

"Thanks to me?" Lisa croaked.

"You told me she had feelings for me, too," he said. "Remember all those hints you gave me that day in the library? We'd spent time together, she was at the barbecue, and she was involved with newspapers."

"Newspapers?" Lisa asked blankly.

Cal gazed at Irina worshipfully. "She's living at the Parker house, and Nanny and her father both work for newspapers."

A pretty far-fetched hint, Lisa thought. But Cal had been primed to fall for Irina. She'd just given him the last little push.

Lisa sighed. Her heart was a little sore, but it would mend. The worst part was that she'd given up her steady beau for a dream that hadn't come true. Jeff Racine would probably never forgive her. Now there were no boys in reserve, and she'd have to start from square one. She hated that.

But tonight she'd seen that there were more important things than boyfriends. The sight of Irina's white face across a crowded ballroom had given her an insight into what real grief was all about.

"Well, I guess we should be going," Zack said, backing out of the office. "Sorry about everything, guys. I guess we let our imaginations run away with us."

"It's okay," Irina said. "We understand."

"We do?" Cal said. "I don't understand anything."

Jessie sighed. "It's been that kind of night."

"It's a full moon," Kelly added. "Weird things happen."

Mark looked at his broken door. "Speaking of weird things," he said. "Don't you guys know how to knock?"

▲　▼　▲

A week later at the Max, the gang gathered to congratulate Screech on his first byline. He had written an article about Irina for the *Gazette*.

"It was great, Screech," Lisa told him. "I cried at the end."

"You really got to me, too," Kelly said. "You made me see that our problems really aren't so important."

"So, Screech, was Nanny impressed?" Slater asked, taking a sip of soda.

Screech nodded. "She couldn't believe I actually wrote it," he said proudly. "She kept asking, 'Do you *swear* you did it all by yourself?'" He sighed. "I'm so happy!"

"And is she over Cal?" Lisa asked. "I know I'm not. Although Toby Welliver asked me out today. He's really cute. I might consider letting him mend my poor little heart."

"That's what I'm going to do for Nanny," Screech declared. "We're going out Saturday night. I realize now that I neglected her, and I won't make that mistake again." He sighed. "I hope she gets over him. She's still pretty sad."

We're all a little sad, Zack thought, surveying the faces at the table. *We all lost at love.*

Kelly and Slater had broken up. He had lost Irina, and because Kelly knew how he'd felt about her, she was still keeping her distance. Jessie and Slater were in their usual state of uncertainty about their relationship. And Lisa had lost both Cal and Jeff Racine.

But they were together. The other night at the ball, the gang had seen that he and Screech had needed help and they'd jumped in without hesitation. That's what made the gang so special.

Jessie raised her glass of soda. "I'd like to make a toast. Here's to Screech's article."

The gang all raised their glasses.

"And here's to friends," Zack said.

Slater, Jessie, Kelly, Lisa, Screech, and Zack clinked glasses.

"Friends forever," they said.

Don't miss the
next HOT novel
about the
"SAVED BY
THE BELL"
gang

OPERATION: CLEAN SWEEP

With everyone suddenly single at Bayside, Zack, Kelly, and Jessie decide it's time to try something desperate: blind dates!

But these blind dates are totally out of control! Is this what has become of dating in the nineties? Find out in the next "Saved by the Bell" novel.